SILICON
SECRETS

Catherine Burr

 New Line Press

To B,
who believed in the dream.

Part One

Foreword

Murder was in the air.

Like a foggy day, it would always be there, hanging over his head; a memory that would not evaporate no matter how hard he tried to erase it. Pressing harder on the gas pedal of his new Ferrari, he was headed for a night in the city.

Glancing at the woman by his side, he wondered what his father would think of him now.

Chapter One

"Get the hell out of my house!"

Lucky Lukovich ducked, narrowly avoiding the empty bottle of wine his father threw at him.

"Pop, stop it."

"You got the devil in you, kid . . . always will."

"I'm warning you, Pop. Don't come near me," pleaded Lucky, who was barely of legal age.

Varic was drunk. Again. Just getting started.

Lucky realized what was in store. He glanced over and saw his father's weapon of choice. A serpent disguised as a leather belt, waiting to strike, hanging on a nail beneath a creased picture of his dead mother.

Lucky remembered the story Sister Anne had told him about the photo, how it was taken on the day he was born in the Slovenian village they called home.

That was the year of the nun's jubilee, so in celebration, they decided to open the gates of their private sanctuary. All parishioners of the coastal town were invited for a picnic behind the convent walls. This was the one and only time they unlocked the gate.

Lucky's mother, Marie, had been excited to be pregnant, and she radiated love that the child within her stirred.

At the picnic, Sister Anne placed her aged hand on Marie's stomach. She breathed in, closing her eyes, and spoke through her heart. "Proof of God's presence."

*   *   *

Over the years, Lucky gazed at that picture hanging on the wall. Longing for her touch, her scent. Love. He wondered what the porcelain-colored flower behind her ear smelled like. What it was called.

In the photo, his mother's auburn hair fell loosely down

her long neck. The color contrasted with the flowing, milky, chiffon dress and the tiny pink rosebuds on her sweater, which was draped over her petite shoulders. Her delicate hands rested on a protruding belly, already proud of the child she would soon give birth to. Marie had gone to the picnic in celebration of the awakening within her heart; an awakening that her pregnancy had brought.

She was smiling, laughing, as she felt the tickling of the baby's movements inside. The moment caught her off guard because she was unaware the camera had clicked right after she'd put the flower behind her ear. That click would be cherished by the yet unborn son she carried, forever.

Sister Anne told Lucky that after the picture was snapped, his mother went into labor. How the two women left the wild blackberry pie and scent of fried chicken still in the air, then raced in a borrowed car to the sterile midwife's house where he was born.

Just a few short years after his mother had died, Sister Anne gave the framed photo to the little boy as a gift he would cherish to his own grave. Sister Anne promised to tell him more about his mother when he was older, but a stroke killed the nun before she could have that conversation. Lucky never knew the details about his mother that he longed for. Never knew why she died, only that he'd been held responsible by his father.

Death took her shortly after his birth. He would never know her, only that her eyes spoke to him from the photo that he said, I love you to every day.

For years now, the meaningful photo had hung on the Lukovich's wall where it still remained, so Lucky could have a connection to the mother he'd never know.

Older and stronger now, Lucky could fight back against his father. Not like when he was a little boy with no control. He still had no mother to protect him, but he could protect himself.

Of course, it wasn't Lucky's fault his mother died when

he was but an infant. Would his alcoholic father ever let him forget?

"You are the reason . . . she is dead," he had said repeatedly, like a chant coming from a choir practice gone bad.

During the days, Varic, who had lost an eye in a bar fight and wore a black patch covering the space where his eyeball should have been, worked as a cobbler. He always smelled of shoe polish and glue. Varic fixed shoes for the locals. Repairing the villager's soles, while dismantling Lucky's soul.

Lucky spent his days ditching the church run high school while snitching candy bars from the local market.

Father and son spent tense nights in a detached garage, for which they paid a small amount of rent to the owners of the house, who had converted the space into squalid living conditions. Sporadic at best, the electricity had been wired unsafely and illegally. Grease stains were in abundance on the concrete slab floor and air circulation was lacking. A leaky roof covered four walls.

With Varic drinking and getting angrier with each swallow, this dwelling often failed to qualify as a home. But this time, after narrowly being missed by the hurled wine bottle, Lucky retaliated with his clenched fist, causing Varic to soar across the plastic-covered sofa, a church donation. He hit the wall in the process, and the cherished photo crashed to the cement floor. Varic landed in the jagged, shattered glass of the wine bottle, the broken picture frame was beneath his bleeding head.

What had Lucky done? The thought horrified him. With trepidation, he looked down at his motionless father. His haunting eye stared into space. Blood dripped down his father's head, his hair clumped together in bloody knots. Lucky trembled as he tugged at the portrait of his beloved mother, now lodged under Varic's motionless self.

"You son-of-a-bitch," Lucky said, wiping the broken chips of glass aside, peeling the picture out, folding it with care, and placing it in his pocket. He would save her and himself. Lucky made an anonymous call to the police, telling them to hurry and get to 64 Rudnick Street, clarifying that it was the garage apartment behind the main house.

And then he ran.

Still wearing the shirt stained with his father's blood, he crouched in the bushes outside a local pub as the speeding police car approached, then disappeared down the street. After he could no longer see the blinking lights of the cruiser, he kept moving. Past the convent. Past the market. Past the cemetery where his mother was buried. Someday he would have enough money to buy her a headstone.

He kept running, the airless night void of answers.

If he had killed his father, he'd be thrown in jail. If he hadn't killed him, his father would see to it that he was held in solitary confinement. Of that, Lucky had no doubt.

Collapsing under a tree, he slept until morning when the swelling of his bruises subsided, but would not be forgotten. These bruises were his life's story.

Squinting from the morning sun, Lucky brushed his black hair, sticky with sweat, out of his brow. He felt his face. A crust of blood must have dried under his right eye where his father's fist met his innocent cheek. The blurring of his eyes caused everything to be a cloudlike cover, but when he focused straight ahead, he saw his destiny.

*   *   *

A ship being loaded with supplies was the answer. The cargo terminal was crowded and bustling with activity. He'd be able to slip by unnoticed. He knew how to get on board, because he had watched the activity on the port since he was a child. Since he was old enough to run from his father. Lucky knew the ship would be headed out of the Adriatic, to the open sea, destined for another country. America perhaps.

As he ran toward the ship, he passed some fishermen, and heard their conversation. "Did you hear about one-eyed

Lukovich?"

"Cops found him. Took him to the hospital. Heard he was dead."

Lucky ran faster, away from the one-eyed man he called Pop, whom even the doctors couldn't save.

Can't believe it, Lucky thought, as he grappled with the news. How many times, he'd wished him dead. And, now he was. Life sucked right out of him by his own hands. The hands of the son. The son who was never called "son" by his old man. If only he'd heard the words even once, but was that reason to kill him? Did abuse justify murder? His father was evil, but he was the only father he'd ever known, ever had. Now, he had no one. Now he was an orphan.

At the end of the pier past the fishermen and buckets of fish waiting to be sold, his fate awaited in the form of a rusty cargo ship. At first, no one saw him sneak on board. The seamen, however, soon discovered him.

"What are yuh running from, kid?" asked Raphael, one of the seafarers. He knew it wasn't uncommon for those running from the law or a woman to try and hitch a ride.

"I'm not running from anything," Lucky lied. "I want to join the crew."

"It's not that easy. You can't just jump on a ship and sail away."

"Why not?"

"Forget the fact that you probably don't have a passport, the paperwork needed to work on board, your shots, any of that. Are you even old enough?"

"I'm a man." If killing someone made you a man, then he passed with flying colors.

"Another thing, Kid, it's not fun in the sun at sea. You can expect long days, even longer nights. You'll go crazy from the tedium, and if sea sickness doesn't kill yuh, the food surely will." The seaman laughed and took a flask from his back pocket, opening it and taking a swig.

"I just want to see the world. And I—" Lucky tried to

remember the swear words he heard on American television shows. "I don't give a shit about the food."

"All you'll see is nothing but sea and sky. For an eternity, it'll seem."

"That would be a break for me." They had no idea how much.

The seamen recognized a desperate soul when he saw one. They were all desperate souls in their own private ways. Taking Lucky in was an easy decision.

"How'd you get the name Lucky?" Raphael asked on the first night at sea, while pouring booze into Lucky's mug.

"Bet I can guess," a drunk voice shouted.

"I used to work at a local market, and I delivered the goods." Lucky smiled as he had the men believing his lies. The truth was irrelevant, out on the vast ocean they wanted fiction, not reality, and he was happy to oblige. Tall tales were the least he could do to repay them for his escape.

During the restless days at sea, he built up his muscles by working out. With each passing day, his body became stronger, yet the emotional scars remained.

The seamen took Lucky in as if he were a lost child at the zoo, but provided him with booze, cigarettes and advice fit for a man. They helped Lucky with his English and taught him American slang. His accent softened by the time they approached U.S. soil.

After its long voyage, the ship pulled into the Port of New York. Lucky hadn't gotten sick once on the trip, and the food was tolerable. When he saw the view of freedom, he wept. With only the crinkled, stained photo of his mother in his pocket, Lucky was a free man.

Chapter Two

"America. Work hard. You'll get rewarded."

"Thanks, guys," Lucky said.

The men had grown to admire Lucky's resolve. They got him through customs by giving him a fake passport. Seamen with cigarettes hanging from their chapped lips wished him luck as he said goodbye to his old life, and hello to his new one.

Lucky hitchhiked into the heart of New York City, where he spent his days in a determined state of mind. He walked through the streets, getting by on discarded food and newspapers to study, visualizing a future with money in his pocket, not to mention a real roof over his head.

He sold his passport on the street for a few bucks. Enough to keep supplied with liquor for a while. The alcohol numbed his brain, temporarily allowing him to fight the image of his dead father, and was his choice of medicine. When he found himself throwing up in a gutter, he walked into the closest building, a doughnut shop.

"Bathroom's for customers only," said the fat, bald-headed guy behind the counter.

"Gotta go," Lucky said, ignoring him, while he ran to the bathroom. He had to yank the warped door a couple of times. And the smell alone, once he got inside, made him throw up even harder. Retching into the plugged up toilet, he felt as if his intestines would be next to come up.

Afterward, he turned the water faucet on. Only a trickle came out, and he cupped his hand under it, rinsing out his mouth with the skimpy amount collected.

Looking at his reflection in the cracked wall mirror, he thought about what the seamen had said. Work hard. You'll get rewarded. That he planned on doing. But first things first. He needed a shower.

When he walked half-stumbling out of the bathroom, he met his next savior.

"You okay, Love Bug?" Dina asked.

He wiped the drips of water from his lips and focused on who was talking to him. Her enormous bosom, teased hair, eggplant-colored spandex pants, and ruby-red stiletto heels brought him back to reality.

After an eternity at sea with a couple dozen men exchanging tales of their onshore escapades, Lucky reached into his pocket to see how much money he had. Two dimes and five pennies were all he had left of the money the seamen had given him.

"My treat." She took a roll of twenty-dollar bills, wrapped together in a rubber band, from her cleavage.

They ate chocolate doughnuts and drank black coffee. By sunrise, he moved in with her and her feisty longhaired mutt, Howard.

*   *   *

The cockroach infested apartment above Corky's Place, an all-night bar where she stripped, wasn't what he had in mind for his life in America, but it was better than the dungeon of his father's house; also better than the cargo ship, and better than the park with too many pigeons. This setting was better than barfing in a backed up toilet in the rear of a doughnut shop, too.

The one room apartment was musty, under-furnished, and had holes in the walls that Lucky could fix.

"I've asked Corky to fix those holes forever," she said. "He just won't."

Lucky stood under the hot water in the shower. He tried to wash the haunting visions of his father away while scrubbing his skin free of the hatred witnessed within his own mind. The hot water soon turned lukewarm, then cold. But his desire to wash away the aching in his heart burned inside, so he remained in the shower, his powerful but weakened hands pressed against the cramped shower wall, his head dropped forward. And he cried.

"Darlin'?" Dina said, pounding on the door to the bathroom. "You've been in there for an hour."

Shit, had it been that long? "I'll be right out."

He dried off with a damp towel that smelled like mildewed tennis shoes.

She'd changed out of her tight pants into a miniskirt and button up blouse. Both clung to her slender body. "I've got a set coming up," she said, taking a drink of something out of a Styrofoam cup and swallowing a pill. "Gotta get downstairs before Corky blows a fuse."

Lucky reached to put his clothes back on. The duds were in a pile, slung over a torn chair that looked as if it were a throwaway. His clothes reeked from barf. "I have to get these washed first," he said, with the towel wrapped around his waist.

"Look in that closet," she said, pointing to a portable clothing rack on wheels. "Take whatever you want. Come downstairs when you're ready. I'll introduce you to Corky. Perfect time to watch me work." Another pill went down her throat.

Following a short nap, Lucky felt the time had come to meet Corky. Not his wish, certainly. Dina'd been so kind to him that he felt obligated.

*   *   *

"What's happening?" Lucky said, extending a hand over the sticky counter top, passing the fast food wrappers to Corky.

Though the bar was dim, there was enough light for Corky to see into Lucky's eyes. Through his years of being a bartender, he thought he knew people well. In the first moments of meeting his gaze, Corky envisioned a wild animal caught in a trap, struggling to escape. Worse than that, he also saw an intruder, someone that hindered his financial plans.

Corky had pulled Dina aside between sets. "I don't like him." His voice was gruff from too many years of smoking cigars and chasing naked broads. "You gotta get ridda him."

She laughed. "You're crazy." She reached under her dress and adjusted the thong. Modest, she wasn't. And she didn't care if a few drunken men saw her. After all, that was how she made her real money. Ignoring Corky's warning, Dina kept the six-foot-two man as her toy. She gave him cash for drinks and smokes.

He sat in the bar night after night, with Jim Beam, smoking and watching Dina dance. He thought her exotic movements were as smooth as the whiskey going down his throat. When drunken, horny men lunged after her, he pushed them aside, demanding respect for his girl.

"Are you out of your mind?" Corky said to Dina. How was he going to get rid of Dina's latest acquisition?

Dina had originally come to New York to join a professional ballet company, but when she hurt her ankle running to catch a subway train, her dancing dreams went from sweet vermouth to whiskey sour overnight. Not wanting to return home to Des Moines where her parents ran a dry cleaner, she opted to stay in New York and take any jobs she could.

Soon, she met Corky at a late night party and he didn't care about her limp. Feet weren't what most of his customers ogled over. He took her in, financing her breast implants. A nose job was on the horizon. Dina lived above the bar, so "part" of her payment came in the form of room and board. Her skills brought in lots of well-paying customers.

When Corky got her loaded, he'd have sex with her in front of a video camera in her apartment and in the back room of the bar. He had cameras strategically located, hidden from view. He planned to continue having sex with her, then sell copies of the tapes over the Internet.

Dina had been growing fond of her new beau, except,

early in the morning, when they went to bed, she found he was restless, often talking in his sleep. She'd have to shake him awake to calm him down.

Corky provided Dina with sleeping pills and other drugs. She wasn't sure what all the different pills did, but they made her dance and sleep with more grace and ease. Without the various chemicals, she wasn't at all sure she could strip night after night.

Having Lucky around was a good thing, even against Corky's demands that he leave. He left, she left.

Dina was having too much fun with Lucky, and they celebrated their friendship with "his and her" tattoos. They got drunk one night and ended up in Greenwich Village where they each got hearts designed. Hers was done in black lettering running through the center of the heart. The words read Lucky. And on his, Dina.

Upon wakening in the morning, Lucky was stunned. Barely did he know her, yet he now had her name stenciled on his arm for life.

"Wait for me upstairs, Lucky. Watch Wheel of Fortune, I'll be back before you know it."

Dina didn't want Lucky in the bar anymore. His presence wasn't worth the killer looks from Corky. Lucky was like a teddy bear, someone to snuggle up with at night. Within his arms she felt safe.

"I got something special for you tonight," Corky said, handing Dina a drink. He spiked it, but she'd never know. Just part of his plan.

After finishing the drink, she felt as if something permeated her blood like smoldering embers. She managed to stumble through her set, then someone grabbed her and took her into a back room.

Corky had extra cameras set up. He was going to make one award winning video before kicking her and Lucky out. When she collapsed on the moth-eaten sofa, he was furious at first. That wasn't in the plan. But he was always thinking.

With her passed out, he could do more than he'd scripted. Elated, Corky grew more and more thrilled with the results.

"You can go home now, Dina," Corky said.

Her head spun as if she'd been forgotten about on a speeding merry-go-round at the fairgrounds. Having eaten nothing, her stomach played tricks on her, telling her she'd eaten too many corn dogs.

"I've got to get home," she whispered, walking with a painful ankle. Had she broken it, again? She stumbled up the stairs leading to her apartment.

Lucky heard the sound of someone climbing the steps. "Is that Mommy?" Lucky said to Howard. The dog walked over to the door. "Want to go meet her?" Opening the door, he expected Dina to enter. When she didn't immediately come into the apartment, the only sound to be heard was TV. Concerned, Lucky peered out the door to see where Dina was, only to find her wavering at the top of the stairs.

She only wore a bra and panties. The smell of cheap rum filled the air. She was barefoot, something completely out of character for her. Her hair was snarled with men's body fluid. She looked like a hyena chasing its next meal, or was it her next fix?

"What drugs did you take?" he asked, grabbing her arm. He was protective, yet angry that she'd been so foolish.

Her eyes were Bloody Mary red. Her lips were quivering. She felt as if her body were on fire as she searched for an extinguisher. "I need water. Put the flames out."

"Get in here," Lucky said, trying to get a hold of her arm.

"Who are you? What's going on?" she asked. Dina pushed him away. "Leave me alone!"

Was she so drugged that she couldn't recognize him? "I'm trying to help you, Dina." She kept slipping away from his grip.

"I'm on fire!" She needed a fireman, and he wasn't help-ing. She screamed, filling the air with a hollow silence as her voice echoed in the night. Pushing Lucky out of the way, she fell backward down two flights of concrete steps, landing at the bottom. Blood began to form on the floor.

"What did you do to her?" Corky said, running to her, out of breath.

"I didn't do anything. I was trying to help her," Lucky said.

Dina was lying on the ground in a fetal position. Not moving. The blood was now a puddle. The dog barked next to her as blood seeped from beneath her head.

That haunting image of his father lying dead replayed in his head. Suddenly, Dina moved. She moaned something he couldn't understand.

"I'm here, babe," he said, kneeling down, causing his black denim jeans to soak up some blood. Taking her hand in his, he stroked the skin on her arms; it was smooth and white, except for the noticeable red needle tracks and tattoo.

"Lucky. Love Bug," she whispered, then closed her eyes. Her body went limp.

"You're going to jail," Corky said, standing over her with a lit cigar clenched between crooked teeth, unaware that ashes were falling on top of her. "I knew you were nothing but trouble. I warned Dina about you." Corky grabbed Lucky's arm and squeezed until it went numb. "Now you're going down, big shot."

The dog bit Corky in the leg, ripping the fabric away from his pants leg.

"I'm gonna kill you," Corky said, kicking the dog furiously as it yelped.

Lucky swung his arm back, finding a place for his fist in Corky's fleshy, splotchy nose. "You-son-of-a bitch." He hit Corky, causing him to fall.

Lucky could hear sirens in the distance. Someone had called the cops. Hopefully an ambulance was on the way.

Dina's fall was an accident. Corky's wasn't. Would the police think he'd pushed her? And him? Would they listen to a man with no ID? A man with blood on his hands? He was an easy target. With Dina unconscious or worse, who knew what lay ahead? Corky was certain to lie to the police when he recovered from a powerful knuckle sandwich. He'd had it in for Lucky during the short time Lucky had been around.

The bar crowd and neighbors who usually minded their own business came out to see what the commotion was about. Lucky didn't understand that, normally no one cared if someone had been stabbed or shot in this rough neighborhood. Why had they decided to start a neighborhood watch now, of all times?

Lucky heard the sirens getting closer. He ran into the apartment, grabbed his backpack that was always kept packed and ready to go. Searching through all the places where he knew Dina hid money, he found none. On his way out the door, with the backpack slung over his shoulder, he saw the dog staring at him. "Shit," he said. "Come on, boy."

The ambulance was just pulling up outside when he and the dog ran out the back alley. He heard someone say, "Lucky did it."

With his good eye, Corky saw Lucky run behind the paramedics, who were rushing around; one with an emergency bag, the other two with a stretcher. Did he think he'd get away that easily?

Managing to pull himself off the ground, Corky limped after him. "I'll kill you." Trying to catch his breath, he was an old man not meant for running down Dina's boyfriends. Out of breath, he leaned over, wheezing. When he looked up, Lucky had vanished.

Chapter Three

There was only one direction for Lucky to go. He had been carrying around a newspaper clipping on Silicon Valley that he'd ripped from the pages of The New York Times. The blueprint for his future was that single page.

He hid out until early morning. Before dawn on the streets, he hot-wired an older Buick model sedan, that wouldn't draw too much attention from cops and pointed it west.

The newspaper article that he had read over and over again, and knew by heart, was entitled, Glory and Gold Rush, focusing on the vast amount of wealth that was being created daily in Silicon Valley. Believing the land of stock options was calling him personally, with Howard at his side and the yellowing article tucked into his flannel shirt pocket, he drove on. He was jubilant when he found cash in the glove box of the stolen car, enough to buy gas and food along the way.

In a week's time, he made good mileage, driving out of the eastern states, through the Midwest, stopping only for necessities.

He phoned several hospitals before tracking Dina down, but the hospital wouldn't release any information about her condition since he wasn't her immediate family.

The two fugitives almost made it through the desert of Nevada when the car started to rattle as if rocks were in the gas tank. Approaching the Nevada-California border, the engine of the stolen car finally gave up its desire to go further. He pushed the car behind a billboard that read, "Visit Beautiful Lake Tahoe."

"Sorry, ol' boy," he said to the dog as he tied him to a post behind the back of a trucker's coffee shop. He thought it would be more difficult to be picked up with an appendage. Anyway, the mutt was becoming a nuisance, always hungry, and looking for a hydrant to relieve himself. A true city animal.

He put on the cowboy hat he'd stolen from a staggering cow brander just in from the range. Flirting with a waitress wearing a mustard-colored polyester uniform and with feet she complained were killing her from working a twelve-hour shift, the cowboy didn't seem to notice his missing hat until Lucky was well down the road, or so Lucky assumed.

Lucky didn't have to wait long for a ride. On the edge of the freeway onramp with his thumb pointed westward, the first big rig stopped for Lucky. Running toward the truck, he tried not to trip over the loose shoelaces hanging down from his tennis shoes.

"Need a lift, do yuh?" the trucker asked, as he turned down the volume of the Reba McEntire CD he had been loudly singing along with.

"I'll go as far as you can take me," Lucky said.

"Hop aboard."

Lucky hesitated.

"Something wrong?"

"Can you wait one minute?"

He ran over to where he tied the dog and quickly let it loose. "Come on, then." The dog followed him, wagging his tail.

"Do you mind?" Lucky asked.

The trucker laughed. "What a pair. Get on in."

Lucky pushed aside a plethora of Mad magazines, Doritos and empty Juicy Fruit gum wrappers as he and the dog climbed in.

Looking at the trucker, he noticed that the creases on the guy's face were as deep as the creases on the cracked vinyl dashboard. He was wearing a baseball cap that was pulled down so tight, it matted his hair around the edges as if he'd been sweating exhaustion from who knows what.

"They call me Potato Sam," he said, taking a slurp from his jumbo-sized coke. When he talked, his belly rolled out over his belt and bounced like a bowl of Jell-O. "Normally, I haul potatoes, but lately I've been working the artichoke run.

I take work where I can get it."

"Lucky's the name," he said, taking off the flannel shirt he had been wearing over a white cotton T-shirt that read "Yankees" on the back.

"Keep it pretty hot in the cab, I know," Sam said, trying to scratch the weariness of the road from his three-day growth of gray whiskers.

"What's the dog's name?"

"Howard."

"My kids are always after me for a dog." Sam was glad for the company of both of Lucky and Howard; it kept him from thinking about his aching back from too many hours on the road.

His wife Edna and four kids, Ginger, Kellie Sue, Caitlin and Sam Junior, were home in Pocatello, waiting for his return. He thought about hugs from his family. A past due notice on his mortgage haunted him, too.

Sam downshifted the gears and the engine howled in response. He drank the rest of the Coke in one gulp and filled his mouth with the melting ice. He rolled the ice around in his mouth so he could speak without sounding as if he'd just gone to the dentist and was still nursing a numb mouth. Then he let the dog slurp the ice remnants out of the cup.

"How far you going?" Lucky asked.

"I'm going as far as Salinas Valley," Sam said.

"I'm headed to Silicon Valley myself."

"Oh yeah? What fer?"

"I hear they hand out stock options like candy."

Sam laughed. "Look, kid, you remind me of a wanna-be actor going to Hollywood with dreams of stardom in yer eyes and sawdust in yer brain. Though Silicon Valley ain't no Hollywood, even still, the sharks'll bite yuh if you let 'em. So be careful."

"With what I've been through in my life, it'll be a piece of cake."

"What are yuh running from, anyway?"

"Nothing. I didn't mean anything." Shit, he shouldn't have said anything. He didn't want to appear suspicious. "I just gotta get to Silicon Valley, it's south of 'Frisco. Are we going near there?"

"First, I ain't going to Silicon Valley." Sam crunched the ice between his coffee-stained teeth. "Second, no one calls the city 'Frisco.'"

"Well, you know, I'm new in town."

"And third," Sam added, like an exasperated school teacher, "everyone in Silicon Valley is new in town."

Lucky felt as if he were back in third grade, being berated by the nuns. "Whatever," he said. He decided to go to sleep.

*   *   *

A few hours later, the truck came to an abrupt stop. "Wake up, kid," Sam said, nudging a sleeping Lucky on the shoulder.

"Thanks, man," Lucky said, jumping out of the cab with his backpack, leaving the cowboy hat behind. The hat had served its purpose, helping him get a ride. Made him a good ol' boy for a few hours. He'd seen enough westerns to know that. "About the dog. Keep him. Give 'em to your kids."

"Hey, man, thanks. Want some chips for the road?" Sam asked, offering him a bag.

Lucky laughed. "That's all right. Which way to the ocean?"

"I thought yuh were headed to the valley?"

"Gotta see the Pacific blue first."

"Take that road all the way till it ends, yuh'll find the paradise you're lookin' for."

"Thanks, see yuh."

"By the way," Sam added, "don't be surprised if the Pacific blue ain't so blue."

Puzzled by his comment, but undeterred, Lucky could

smell the salt air of the ocean. He walked down the darkened road. Short bushes lined either side of the almost vacant road, and the crickets sang an opera. Lucky followed the scent and taste of salty air, passing through waxy ice plants that grabbed at and tickled his legs.

The moon glowed in the reflection off the water. Waves were gentle sounding as if they had gone to sleep for the night. Wondering where all the people were, he thought the beach had an eerie silence. Resting next to the glow of a smoldering bonfire, he fell asleep on the soft-as-cotton-balls, warm sand.

Not long into the night, the once inviting sand became cold and damp.

He struggled in his sleep. Dina. Whatever happened to her? Had she died? He shouldn't have left her, but he was scared.

His dream turned to brutal visuals of his father. "No, stop, stop," he pleaded, waking himself. Would no one help a little boy? Rolling around on the granules beneath him, he fought an invisible enemy. He didn't know where he was. But the darkness felt as if he had been locked in a closet. The memory of that so real dream caused him to tremble.

"Because of you, she's dead."

That horrid voice taunted him, never leaving him in peace, even when asleep. Someone would help him escape. Bring him into the light. Save him from his father's treacherous hand. He shouldn't have killed him; that was wrong, but the man deserved to die, didn't he?

Shivering, he felt a presence. Had she come to save him? "Mom—ma!" he cried out.

*   *   *

"Rise and shine," a voice said.

Wiping the fine grains of sleep out of his eyes, he looked up and saw a curly-haired man with mirrored sunglasses staring at him. He was wearing a brightly colored Hawaiian shirt, shorts and tennis shoes. Lucky wondered if he was being mugged, which he thought was funny, since he didn't have any cash.

"No overnight sleeping on the beach," the man said. Every morning he had to clear the transients before the tourists rolled in; appearance was everything in a tourist town.

"I don't have any money," Lucky said.

The man laughed as he extended his hand.

"I can get up myself," Lucky said, standing up.

"I'm Officer Thomas."

"Officer?"

"That's right." Thomas knew from experience that people always did a double take when they saw the police dressed so casually. When the city first adopted the casual attire code, he wasn't quite convinced, until he realized how much more comfortable the loose-fitting shirts were.

Lucky noticed a badge on his shirt, but it was embroidered directly onto the shirt. He shook his head in disbelief. In his sleep, he'd been in a black hole, but woke up in paradise.

This officer was friendly and was dressed for a luau. He didn't look all businesslike, as the officers back home did who Lucky feared were waiting to beat him into a murder confession. Heck, he was a far cry from resembling the officers in New York who waited to arrest him on a bogus assault charge.

Maybe they would make him confess his mother's murder too; after all, his dad was convinced that he'd killed her before even getting a chance to know her. To hear her voice. To tell her he loved her. To feel her motherly arms around him. To breathe the scent of the flower behind her ear.

"Move along now, son."

"No problem," Lucky said, wiping the sand off his pants.

"Son, you can go clean up over there in the bathroom." He pointed to a small, square building, the size of Lucky's former house. A sign on the shack read, "Public Restrooms." There were drinking fountains next to the building, a row of outdoor showers and a rack filled with bikes.

"Thank you," Lucky said. He knew coming to California was a good idea, and he was glad the night was over. He hated the darkness. The daylight erased the night demons that tortured him so much.

After using the public toilets, he enjoyed walking through the misty fog toward the ocean. The water was gray. Now he knew what Sam's words meant. He laughed. Walking over to a barbecue pit, he picked up a charred hot dog from a metal grill. The hot dog was cold, but he didn't care. It would be a feast.

Sitting on a piece of driftwood that seemed like a king's throne, he breathed out the pain and inhaled the fresh air that soon filled his lungs with hope.

He set the hot dog on his lap and pulled a cigarette out of his pack. The smokes were crushed from where he'd fallen asleep on them. Taking out the last light from a Corky's Place matchbook, he lit his bent cigarette. Maybe he should quit. The thought lasted for only a split second before he disregarded that notion as ridiculous. Smoking in clean air was refreshing, even if his lungs burned in the process.

The endless repetition of the waves mesmerized him. They were hypnotic. Each one unique. Each one with its own personality. Its own symphony.

Multiethnic seagulls, gray, white, and mixed colors flew in formation overhead. Their wings were flapping, but they appeared as if not even moving. They were singing high-pitched songs in short bursts that echoed through the fog, private conversations with each other while surveying the morning buffet of picnic leftovers. The seagulls on land hopped on toothpick-thin legs, their beaks pecked at the sand, hunting for breakfast.

Lucky buried the remnants of his cigarette with the toe of his tennis shoe, and ate his breakfast of one cold, rubbery hotdog. Not quite the feast he'd imagined it to be.

Heavy fog that had been hugging the ocean evaporated. Just like that. At first the water was gray, then blue with white foam lapping gently on shore. An ever-changing kaleidoscope of color.

The sky was now cloudless and the sun's warmth embraced him . . . as his mother would have, had he not killed her.

People began to appear on the beach. Joggers first, then sun-worshippers with towels, sunscreen, backrests, radios and ice chests on wheels. The day transformed in front of him. An artist's masterpiece.

He had fallen in love with the mysterious color-changing ocean. The soft sand. The indecisive fog. It was paradise.

Now that he'd seen the Pacific, he needed to get to the valley. He'd planned to revisit this utopia often, but first had to claim his gold mine.

A dog, golden in color with a navy blue bandanna around his neck, ran past him, headed for a Frisbee that had just flown by. A blonde vision ran by, trailing behind the frisky dog.

"Winslow . . . Winslow — here, boy. Come here," she yelled as she reached behind to grab her falling bathing suit straps. "Winslow, here, boy!"

The more she called, the more the dog ignored her. She tried whistling, but he didn't respond to her high-pitched sound.

"Looks like you could use some help," Lucky said, running to catch up to her. He thought she appeared to be floating through the sand, a gazelle through a spring-time meadow.

The girl stopped for a moment as she finished retying her bathing suit straps around her neck. She glanced at the guy offering to help. He seemed to be about her age, but didn't have the surfer-boy hair or the saggy, knee-length board shorts. There was no surfboard in one hand or skim board in the other. He wore long pants, but worse than that, tennis shoes and socks. On the beach, a sure sign of a foreigner.

"No, I don't need any help," she said. What did he think she looked like, a little girl in pigtails who had lost her puppy?

Her Golden Retriever was no puppy, and it wasn't lost, just gotten away. The pooch ran passed the tow-hair kids to chase the pelicans and seagulls that were swooping up hot dog bun fragments. The seagulls scattered, so Winslow ran past the birds into the foamy waves breaking onto the shore.

"Winslow, get back here!"

Lucky ignored her standoffishness. "Why not let him be?" he asked, looking into her sunny Mediterranean-blue eyes.

"See those lifeguards over there?"

Lucky looked at the muscle men. Standing on a balcony on top of aqua-colored wooden towers perched in the sand, they scanned the beach with yellow binoculars.

"That sucks. I'll get him for you."

"That's really not necessary, but if you want to, go ahead."

She sat on the sand and waved to an older woman wearing a caftan, doing her morning yoga exercises. Wanda was her seventy-year-old next-door neighbor, who was on the beach every day, rain or shine.

"Got him," Lucky said, tugging at the soaked bandanna around Winslow's neck.

"Thanks," she said to the guy who was so persistent.

The dog, with his solid muscular build, jumped up on her, licking her face with his affectionate tongue. She started laughing. "Winslow, you are a handful."

Lucky sat next to her, uninvited. He couldn't tear his gaze from hers. Her eyes emanated strength and vulnerability at the same time. "I know the dog's name, what's yours?"

"Heather. Heather Kane."

"I'm Lucky."

"Lucky for what?"

"Lucky to meet you, I think," he said, petting the dog with the wagging tail and a smile and showing his long, sharp white teeth.

Laughing, she watched him with her dog. He was good-looking in a different sort of way. Dark eyes with matching hair. Bronze-color skin, but not necessarily from being tan. She had never seen him on the beach before and wondered where he was from.

"You got all wet," she said demurely, noticing his short-sleeved T-shirt was no longer white, but transparent and clinging to his muscular chest.

"My pleasure." And he meant it. Lucky thought her voice sounded as if she was a soul filled with kindness and love, her face soft and gentle. "Besides, I won't melt. It'll dry in no time."

He tried to glance at her body without overtly staring. Each yellow triangle of her bikini top just barely covered her gently emerging breasts. She was diminutive, and enchanting.

"Winslow doesn't like the busy season here. I'm supposed to keep him leashed; California law. But during the winter, the tourists are gone and the lifeguards move south, it's much different then, the people are gone.

"You should see winter here, it's beautiful. The weather is clear and warm. Frankly, it's a little secret we locals don't let on to the tourists about."

"Too bad, I'm gonna miss that. Don't plan on staying that long. Just passing through."

Heather took a rubber band from the front pocket of her fringed blue jean shorts and tied back her natural sun-bleached hair. Her loose ponytail fell seductively down a slender back, which Lucky longed to caress. Her skin glowed as if flecks of gold shimmered from it in the newly bursting sun.

Lucky couldn't take his eyes off her. She had such innocent eyes, and sun-loved hair.

"It was nice to meet you," she said. "I've gotta get home and get ready for work." She put a collar around the dog's neck, over top of the bandanna.

"Yeah, see you around."

Heather started to walk away, but Winslow tugged at the leash back toward Lucky.

"Come on, boy," she said, but the dog didn't budge. She'd had Winslow since he was a puppy, after he'd strayed through the neighborhood for days. She kept him ever since.

Looking back at Lucky, she thought he seemed not just alone, but there was something in his eyes that spoke to her. His eyes appeared to be telling her something, but what? Wondering if she could trust him, she thought about inviting him back to her place. "Feel like breakfast?" she asked, surprising herself. She couldn't believe the words came out of her mouth.

"Yes," he said. Lucky couldn't believe his good fortune; the girl was more than a passing vision. She was real, and she had extended him an offer impossible to refuse.

They stopped at the outdoor shower stalls where she washed off the sand, which seemed to be a second skin. She carried her sandals, walking barefoot.

"What's your real name?" Heather asked.

"I've been Lucky for as long as I remember."

"That's funny." He was being serious, and she thought he was joking.

The trio crossed the street, walking through a parking lot that was filling up fast with anxious beach goers, no doubt wanting to get the best available space. Mistakenly, they probably believed that one spot over another got better sun.

"It's up there." Heather pointed to a row of cottages on a narrow street. "I live in one side of one of those houses, in a duplex," she explained.

Rusted vans with surfboard racks lined the street out front, in the middle of which was a new car, a Volkswagen convertible.

"Look at that car," Lucky said, laughing. "Someone's painted flowers on it." He glanced inside; the daisies in a test-tube-sized vase in the dashboard matched the daises on the outside. "Must've been custom."

"That's my bug," Heather said, shrugging her shoulders as she took Winslow's leash off.

"It's got a manual transmission?"

"Yeah, you know how to drive stick?"

"No, I'd like to learn though."

"It's easy. My house is right here," Heather said.

Lucky thought the dwelling was a hideous color, an avocado green with purple trim. He wondered how long it had been since it had been painted. "This is nice," he lied.

Perched atop a leaning, wooden post out front, a mailbox jetted out from the cracked sidewalk. The mailbox itself was covered with seashells.

"I did that myself," she said, proudly, noticing him looking at it. She couldn't help a small giggle. "Do you mind taking your shoes off, Lucky?"

He noticed an out of control cinnamon-colored bougainvillea growing up alongside the peeling stucco. There were several potted plants and a windsock decorated with a sailboat hanging from a nail on a beam above the small front porch. Bamboo shades covered the two picture windows in the front.

Removing a key from under a clay pot covered with moss and filled with tangerine-colored geraniums, she unlocked the front door. There was a wreath on the door made of dried flowers, which swished when the door opened.

"You can leave your backpack out here," she said, pointing to a wicker chair with chipped white paint that graced the front porch.

Lucky left his backpack there as requested and followed her into the duplex. "Nice place," he said, looking around, breathing in the sweet aroma of the room. Was that perfume?

"You can sit there," she said, pointing to a sofa that was covered with a khaki slipcover. Floral printed pillows brought color to the room. The room, while feminine, was earthy, just as Heather seemed to be.

He pushed aside a crocheted blanket that was draped over the back of the sofa, sat down, and stretched out.

"Something smells good," Lucky said.

"Thanks. Listen, do you mind if I make lunch instead of breakfast? I like to have a sandwich before I go to work."

"That would be great."

"Vegetarian, all right?" she said, more of an announcement than a choice. She went into the kitchen, a small room adjacent to the living room.

"Sure," he lied.

"I'm not a perfect vegetarian, but red meat is out. Local fishermen bring in catches, so I eat fish. What kind of herbal tea would you like?"

"Know what? Cold water is fine."

"Nothing in it?"

"Sometimes a thirsty guy just wants plain ol' water." He laughed.

She laughed too, as a warmth came over her.

"What's this?" he asked, looking at a painting of the seashore with a scampering dog and young children at play. "This is pretty good."

"Oh, that," Heather said. "That's nothing. Just a painting I did." She was carrying a tray of sandwiches, steaming herbal tea for her, and a glass of water, which she had adorned with a wedge of lemon. She set the tray down on a small table. "You like jazz?" she asked, walking over to a stereo.

Lucky didn't know about jazz, but he was grateful for what was before him. Someday he'd be eating steak and eggs, not whole wheat bread filled with alfalfa sprouts, tomatoes and cucumbers.

"Where do you live?" she asked between bites.

"On the road, mostly."

"That must be rough," she said, glancing at the scar under his right eye, wondering if he'd been in a fight or an accident.

"I'm gonna settle down soon in the valley."

"Oh, Los Angeles?"

"No, Silicon."

"Looking for your pot of gold, huh?"

"Something like that."

"Want another sandwich?"

"No, I'm good," Lucky said, realizing how relaxed he was feeling. He began to think of delaying his Silicon journey. Maybe he would be a beach bum for a while. His whole life was ahead of him as was his opportunity to become a mogul. And he liked being with her, even if she was a vegetarian.

"Must be great living so close to the beach."

"It is. Sea Breeze is a perfect place to live. The air is clean, the people are real and the rent is cheap."

"It is?"

"Well, it is compared to Silicon Valley. Listen," Heather said, "I've gotta get ready."

"Your boyfriend coming over?"

"No, no, I just meant I have to get ready for work. Make yourself at home. I won't be long. You have a girlfriend?"

Dina was no girlfriend. "No," he said.

She'd warmed up to him and almost felt sorry for the guy who seemed a little lost. He had come to California thinking he would find riches, but didn't even have a place to live. He obviously didn't have a car and probably no money. Nothing in the way of clothes, either, she surmised. Plus, she wasn't sure if he even knew where Silicon Valley was located. Why else would he end up at the beach? The valley was on the other side of the hill, almost a country away in many ways.

While she was in the shower, he checked out the rest of the duplex. Glancing in the bedroom, he noticed it was blue, even the ceiling, though it had white clouds painted on it. The dog, wagging his tail, followed him everywhere.

Walking into the kitchen, he noticed she had placed the dishes in the sink, and for a second he thought about washing them, but quickly dismissed the thought. He noticed a crystal bowl with three white flower blossoms floating in it on the kitchen table. The flowers seemed familiar.

He ran to get his backpack from the front porch. Going back into the kitchen, he took the picture from a zippered pocket. Looking at the photo, then back at the flowers on the table, he was stunned. The same delicate flower that adorned his mother's hair. That day at the picnic. The day he was born.

He slowly breathed in the scent, filling his lungs with the fragrance he'd longed to know and had always ached for. The scent of his mother.

"Why?" he whispered. Tears clouded his vision. Why had God let his mother die? Because he killed her. His penance was living with his demonic father. The man had to be done away with. But he didn't really mean to kill him. He just wanted him silenced for a while.

Heather walked into the kitchen. "What are you doing, Lucky?"

"Nothing." Wiping his eyes, he quickly folded the picture and hid it in his pants pocket. "I think I got sand in my eyes." Wiping the moisture away didn't ease the aching inside. That pain would never go away.

"Don't rub too hard, you'll scratch your cornea."

"I'll be careful." Looking at her, he realized how nice it was to have someone who cared about him. She was wearing a terry cloth bathrobe, the color of a yellow canary, with the letter "H" embroidered in green on the front. But, it wasn't that which caught his attention. Nor was it her flawless face, unhindered by make up. There was an aura around her being.

"What are you looking at?" she asked. His staring made her uncomfortable.

"Nothing." He shook his head. "Actually, I was wondering about these flowers. What are they?"

"Why?"

"No real reason."

"In that case, I'm gonna go get dressed," she said, wondering what his real story was. What was he hiding? "About the flowers, they're gardenias. A friend of mine gave those to me."

Lucky's heart sank. "Your boyfriend?"

Heather laughed. "Oh, no, no. It's not like that. Robbie's just a friend. A good friend. We work together. Say, maybe you'll meet him sometime."

"I'd like that." What the hell was he saying? He had plans to make, places to go. He didn't want to get involved, but this girl had cast a spell on him.

"Where are you from anyway? Your accent?"

"I'm from across the pond. A small country in central Europe. I lived near the coast too. I love being near the water."

"You'd like it here then."

"I got other plans."

"Your English is good."

"I spoke English growing up, the nuns insisted."

"Nuns?"

"It's a long story."

"I'd like to hear it, but unfortunately, I don't have time right now. I'll be right back," she said, leaving the kitchen.

"Take your time."

After she left the room, he removed one of the gardenia blossoms out of the bowl, then took the photo from his pocket. He was sure that the flower was the same type that had adorned his mother's beautiful hair. He closed his eyes as he breathed in the fragrant scent. Now Lucky held it in his fingers. The wanting memory. The flower was as sweet as he always knew it would be. Just like his mother.

"Momma," he whispered.

Tears came without invitation. Breathing was difficult. Slumping into the kitchen chair, he felt faint, thinking perhaps he'd been on the road too long. He didn't think he'd ever be able to move from the chair.

"You, okay?" Heather asked as she came back into the room, still wearing the robe, but now her hair was out of the towel, though still damp.

"I think I'm getting a cold," he said, turning his head away from her, wiping the tears away that had dripped down his cheeks. The urge to get up and run as fast as he could out of the duplex and down the street washed through him. The beach was the place he longed to be. He'd be left alone there amongst the crowd. He could think through and relive his memories. Or lack of them.

"If you're getting a cold, better take some Vitamin C."

"No, that's all right," he said as he stuffed the blossom and the photo into his pants pocket. He'd just made an ass out of himself in front of the most beautiful girl he wanted to know more about. In many ways, he felt as if he already knew her.

"Here you go," Heather said, handing him a bottle of orange-colored tablets and a box of tissue. "I just gotta do my hair. You can look through my CD's, if you want."

He took the picture and gardenia blossom from his pocket, put them into his backpack, and turned his focus to the music collection.

Of course, he didn't recognize any of the artists, with names like Slightly Stoopid, Reel Big Fish and Wally's Swing World.

"Do you work fulltime?" Lucky asked, loud enough so she could hear, but all he could think about was the hole in his heart.

"I'm taking summer school at the community college, but during the year, I go to the nearby State University. And I work part-time as a hostess at Chez Von."

"Chez, who?" he asked.

"It was Chez von Trier originally, but over time, it just became known as Chez Von. It's French. The power lunch crowds utilize expense accounts."

"That's nice," he said, thinking if he were married to her, she wouldn't have to work and would have time to explore her artistic side. He'd support her financially and emotionally.

"Anyway," she said. "It's on other side of The Hill. It's a bit of a drive, but it's worth it 'cause the tips are great."

"The hill?" Lucky asked.

Heather laughed. "That's right, you're new here. Let me explain, The Hill is what separates us from them. It's another world over there. The world that you want to claim."

The duplex was warm with the sun streaming through the living room window. Deciding not to play any music, he opted to turn on the TV set instead.

"Amazing," he said, stunned by her fresh beauty as she came into the room. He couldn't take his eyes off of her. She glowed more than before. He had to get a grip. At this rate, he'd never make it to the valley, but at this moment, he didn't care.

Wearing a sleeveless, chiffon-like dress that stopped just above her knees, she looked good. Heather's hair was now fully dried and shining. She still didn't have makeup on, except for a hint of pink lipstick.

"You look beautiful," he finally managed.

Heather blushed. "Thanks, I have to dress up, I'm a hostess there, so you know."

Actually Lucky didn't know, but he wanted to.

"Thanks for everything," he said as he headed for the front door.

"Where are you going?"

While showering, she'd already decided that he could stay if he wanted. The relationship would be platonic. He could sleep on the sofa. She was a virgin who wasn't going to have sex until marriage. But, there was something about him that made her not want to see him go away. Something about his eyes, a longing that filled her as nothing ever had.

"I was gonna shove off."

"How are you going to get there? Don't you need a ride?"

A ride? He didn't even know where he was going to stay, let alone how he was going to get there. He just knew he needed to keep moving.

"I can drop you off somewhere. Or I have a better idea, you can stay here, if you want." She blurted it out, without reservation.

"Really? You don't even know me."

"I think I do."

He accepted her invitation to stay. She had a substance that couldn't compete with stock options or glory and gold. And since he didn't own much of anything, moving in with her was easy.

The gentle town of Sea Breeze would now be his home.

When Heather had gone to work, he called Corky's Place, asking for Dina.

"She's still in the hospital," Corky had said. The noise of the music in the bar must have drowned out any recognition that it was Lucky calling.

A relieved Lucky asked, "She's okay then?"

"Who is this? Turn the music down," Corky yelled to someone.

Lucky hung up.

*   *   *

During the rest of the summer, the beach was filled with well-oiled bodies of every shape and color. Children ran with sand buckets filled with dying sand crabs that they tried to sneak home as souvenirs from their day at the beach. Wanda did her yoga and strolled up and down the beach with her visiting grandkids. The boardwalk amusement park was filled with people of all shapes and sizes, from divorced parents with their kids to young lovers on a first date.

Off in the distance the sea lions sprawled under the wharf barked, amusing locals and tourists alike.

*   *   *

"Don't you have any family?" Lucky asked Heather.

Why hadn't anyone ever come to visit?

"I'm an only child, and I ran away from home. It just got to be too much."

"I understand." Only too well.

"After I left home, I was homeless for a while, but then I found this place."

Lucky thought he could relate to Heather more than ever.

*   *   *

"Who is that woman?" Heather asked, removing a picture and a dried flower she saw in a drawer when she was putting his clean clothes away after a shopping trip they'd made together. She'd bought him clothes at a thrift shop.

Burgundy wine-like splotches blurred the dark-haired woman in the photograph. But Heather could tell she was beautiful. Her eyes were enchanting, strong, yet vulnerable. On the back of the photograph was written, Marie.

"She's my mother, leave it alone," Lucky said, snapping like a cracked crab. This piece of paper was all he had of her. All he ever knew. The flower was the only scent. Beyond that, he would never let Heather or anyone else inside his private world.

*   *   *

The novelty of living near a beachside carnival soon wore off. Piercing screams coming from joyfully excited roller coaster riders, soon started to annoy Lucky.

There was always the sound of the traffic on the street, from the unwelcome valley day timers in their SUV's, to the backfiring of rusty vans with shaky surf board racks on top, to harried tourists in rental cars with headlights stuck in the on position, even during the brightest of days. Some cars seemed to park on their street for no reason at all. Coming down the sidewalk in front of their duplex were kids with rainbow-colored hair on skateboards, and grannies on bicycles. The endless irritation of the boardwalk rides in the distance made him want to find the plug and pull it like a bathtub stopper.

The area quiets down in the winter, Heather had said.

But until then, Lucky felt that, even through the noise, the bohemian community was charming in its own way, as if happily stuck in a nineteen-sixties time warp. Senior citizens, who had once called themselves hippies, ate doughnuts and drank black coffee while reminiscing about Grateful Dead concerts. They passed down the art of tie-dyed T-shirts to the younger generation and smoked marijuana while shopping for Birkenstocks on the net.

Still, Lucky thought it was better living in this coastal town with Heather, who brought him beer, than it was living in the bug infested apartment over Corky's bar with stripper Dina, especially since he'd needed to leave New York fast.

He spent his days on the beach, reading business journals, magazines and papers. Anything that mentioned Silicon Valley. When he wasn't on the beach, he was researching high-tech companies on the Internet on Heather's computer. He'd decided that soon he'd make the drive away from the beach, over the hill, and stake his claim. In the meantime, while Heather was in the fantasy world of college lectures, he was in the real world classroom, but without the expense of tuition.

Heather adored his dark soulful eyes and felt safe embraced in his muscular arms. He was her live-in protector. Her girlfriends were jealous, she could tell from their gestures at the mention of his name. Where had she found him? They wanted to know.

Coyly, she told them where she'd found him in a single word. "Around." Explaining, she thought of him as just a very good friend. They hadn't seemed to believe her when she told them it was platonic. But Heather knew the truth. He had become much more. Not sexually, but intimately. He'd become part of her life, like a warm embrace upon waking, something she no longer wanted to live without.

When he wasn't lifting weights, Lucky played volleyball on the beach, ran, talked to fishermen who always had stories to tell, and he had afternoon tea with Wanda, while she extolled the virtues of meditation. He waited for Heather to come home from school or work, surprising her by having washed the dishes and laundry.

Heather taught him how to drive her car. He picked up driving a stick shift in no time. The car was good on gas mileage and got them where they needed to go.

Lucky would do thoughtful things like bring Heather her favorite peanut butter saltwater taffy from the wharf. He massaged her shoulders after she'd been up all night working on a paper for one of her classes.

But she heard desperation in his voice after darkness descended. She'd come into the living room, sit with him on the sofa, and hold him tight because he trembled in his sleep. He cried out in a language she didn't understand. She wiped droplets of moisture from his forehead with her hand, being careful not to scratch his face with the dangling bracelets of miniature crystal beads that she'd strung together with dental floss.

Gently stroking his brow, she wondered how he got the tiny scar beneath his right eye. She'd kiss it gently while he slept. Outlining the tattoo on his upper arm with her fingers. She wondered who Dina was, but Heather vowed to never pry.

In the morning, before he was fully awake, his gaze looked to her for the acceptance he'd never had before.

They celebrated the end of the summer season with a picnic on the beach, talking deep into the night. Fresh crab. French bread and a gallon-sized bottle of chilled Chablis. As the sun voyaged further west, summer ended.

He opened his heart as he'd never expected to do. Without sex, they had time to talk, exchange ideas, and cuddle on a soft blanket while their backs floated on the soft warm sand and the universe opened up in the sky. They watched the black heavens give birth to the stars of the Milky Way.

"I love the evenings," Lucky said, pouring Heather another glass of wine.

"It's quiet after the tourists have gone home. I love this time of year because of the peaceful silence," Heather said, her head on his chest.

"This was the best summer I've ever had," Lucky said. Heather distracted him from his ultimate goal, and his biggest fear was that he'd fallen in love.

Walking back to the house from the beach after their picnic celebration, they held hands. Winslow followed alongside.

At the house, Heather went into the bathroom while Lucky stepped into the kitchen.

"Want some more wine?" Lucky shouted.

"Maybe just a bit."

He poured two glasses of chilled white wine, set them on the makeshift coffee table, and turned on some soft jazz music, which he'd come to appreciate. Then, he went into the bedroom and lit vanilla-scented candles in preparation for what he'd hope the night would bring. Returning to the living room, he waited.

"Come here," he said as she came out of the bathroom. She'd changed into an oversized T-shirt of his, with only panties underneath. Her sun-tinted legs were bare all the way to her toes.

Sitting on his lap, she pulled his T-shirt off over his head. His pecs were strong and comforting. She ran her finger over each sculpted muscle of his chest.

"It's been a great summer, hasn't it?" she asked, her fingers caressing his cheeks, stopping under his right eyebrow. She moved closer to him and brushed her lips against the small scar.

"It's been the best summer of my life," he said. He put his arm behind her, drawing her into to him.

The gesture made her feel safe, secure, but most of all, loved. She tilted her head and rested on his shoulder, loving the cuddling, not wanting it to ever end. She loved the way their bodies fit together when he had his arms around her.

"Let's have a toast," he whispered, breaking the silence. Picking up the glasses, he handed her one. "Ready?"

"You mean for the toast?" She was ready for more. He'd been patient, never trying anything more than kissing. They'd agreed in the beginning to be friends, their relationship platonic, and it had been, until now. She'd always told herself she'd save herself for marriage, but this man, she would marry. She'd spend the rest of her life with him.

They held the two glasses up in the air.

"Heather?"

"Yes?"

"Love you."

Tears filled her eyes. "I love you, too," she said, adding, "here's to forever."

They sipped the wine, then Lucky took her glass and set it in on the table next to his. Leaning toward her angelic face, he knew the inevitable had happened. He was in love.

Picking her up, he carried her into the bedroom, where the room was filled with an aura, in the soft candlelight. The dog followed, then turned around and went back to the living room where he jumped up on the sofa.

"You are the best thing that has ever happened to me," she said, as Lucky gently placed her on the bed.

Still wearing the T-shirt, she crawled under the blankets with only her head showing. Her first time, she should've been more nervous, but he was so gentle, so loving. She was ready.

"What are you doing?" he laughed.

"I'm waiting for you."

He hadn't pushed her, and now the time was right. Crawling in next to her, he tugged her shirt off over her head, exposing her bare breasts.

"Do you have protection?" she whispered. She pulled her panties off and tossed them to the floor.

Lucky got out of bed, and went to his wallet, taking out a condom. Ready, he jumped back into bed, causing the mattress to bounce.

She laughed.

"What is so funny?" he asked, teasing her.

"You are," she said, reaching her hands around his neck, her legs around his torso, pulling him close to her.

They tossed playfully around on the bed, giggling and savoring every moment, then the mood became more serious. Running his fingers over her chest, he cupped them around her breasts, leaning down to kiss them. Her nipples hardened as his tongue darted gently.

Thrusting his hips, they were harmonious. He was fulfilled at the moment she conveyed her uncontrollable chills to him. Quickly, the chills were chased away by heat and perspiration. Her first time would be a wonder, she was certain. But this surpassed all of her expectations. "I love you," she whispered, holding him tight, her arms wrapped around his neck, her legs around his torso.

"Love you too," he said, kissing her salty face. "What did you want to talk to me about earlier?"

"I forgot." She had the words in her mind, but now they were forgotten. Only their heartbeats could be heard with clarity. And they were beating I love you.

Soon, she drifted off to a peaceful sleep, happy, serene, and content.

In the morning, he surprised her with a tray, brought to the bed, filled with tea, toast and fresh strawberries from the corner market. "How are you feeling?" he asked.

Putting her arms to rest behind her head, she smiled. "Fantastic."

After breakfast, they made love again. By supper, Heather knew it was time for them to start the rest of their lives together. He was her soulmate, together, forever.

*   *   *

At Chez Von, she asked her boss a favor. That night when she came home, she surprised Lucky with the news as she came into the house carrying a bag of fresh artichokes. "I got you a job."

"Oh?" He filled a pot with water to boil the artichokes. He wasn't entirely surprised. All along, he'd planned on finding a job. His first step to taking over Silicon Valley. Now what he needed was a fake identification card.

"It's just a busboy position. But, there's room for advancement. You could be manager one day."

"Heather, I don't have a birth certificate. No driver's license."

"Oh, they don't care about that. Besides, you can get a fake driver's license at the flea market."

The thought of working in a restaurant, especially one that catered to the wealthy of the valley, was the last thing he wanted to do, but this could be a start.

"Now we can always be together."

At first Lucky was pissed over her uninvited plans for him. This was his life, he would set the wheels in motion in his own way.

"I guess I'll give it a try." He decided the job might work out, but only until his chance came for the kind of advancement he had in mind.

*   *   *

Lucky's job as a busboy was short lived. Soon he advanced to waiter and the pay jump was phenomenal because of tips. Heather was right about the tips.

Heather was pleased. Her life was perfect, almost.

Chapter Four

"There's something I want to talk to you about," Heather said, from inside the bathroom, as she heard Lucky coming into the duplex. The front door shut. She was staring at her reflection in the mirror. Her freckles always bothered her, and her nose was too small. She took a deep breath as she waited for Lucky to answer.

Lucky leaned down to pet Winslow and the dog met his face with a slobbery kiss.

"Oh, yeah?" he asked Heather, walking into the kitchen. He opened the fridge with the burned out light bulb inside, took out an ice-cold beer, and went into the living room.

Plopping down on the couch, he turned on the TV. Winslow followed. The dog had a tennis ball in his mouth and was ready for action.

"You got dinner ready?" Lucky asked, his voice loud.

"Not, yet," she said through the walls.

Lucky laughed, then asked Winslow. "You want a sip?"

The dog did respond by dropping the ball and opening his mouth. Lucky poured some beer inside.

As he clicked through all the channels, he found nothing that interested him and turned the set off.

Winslow, after returning with the ball, jumped off the couch and waited by the front door, his tail wagging, sweeping the dust off the hardwood floor with each swoosh.

"Later fella," Lucky said, setting the empty beer bottle down. He got up to get another brew, but was interrupted by Heather's beauty. She'd entered the room.

"What were you talking about?"

"Forget it."

Scooping her off her feet, her ninety-nine cent rubber thongs fell off. "You are glowing," he said. Quickly, he carried her into their bedroom and laid her on the twin bed where they made love and slept squeezed together every night.

Pulling her denim cutoff shorts down her bronzed legs, he heard a wailing siren outside. A jogger probably had a heart attack, or perhaps a cop was chasing a drug dealer.

"This place is so noisy," he complained. When he became rich, he'd buy her a quiet house, away from the noisy street.

"Forget about it." She wrapped her legs around his waist. "It's quieter than before."

He wiggled loose, getting up from the bed, taking a sip of water from a glass that had been sitting on the nightstand for several days.

"Something wrong?" she asked. She understood that he'd seemed distracted. Fixing that would be easy. He needed to focus, that's all.

"I'm fine," he said. "Later, okay?" He leaned over and took a cigarette from a pack he kept in the nightstand.

"That's one habit you have to get rid of. One thing you'll learn about California, is people just don't smoke here."

"Oh, they don't, huh? What do they do then, chew gum?"

"Not a bad idea, I'll get you some," she said, giggling.

Lucky leaned down and gave her a kiss. "I'm going for a walk." For a smoke, he meant.

"Okay, I'll get dinner ready."

"Sounds good," he said, walking out of the house, with the dog trailing behind.

With a lit cigarette dangling from his mouth, Lucky took Winslow down to the beach, where he could smoke in peace. She discouraged his habit and wanted him to quit, but that was unthinkable. Smoking was a birthright to a European.

The sun, a blazing fireball, soon set deep into the eternal horizon.

Since summer had ended, Lucky noticed that the fog left

with it, leaving the days warmer than they'd been. Heather was right about that. The fog played cat and mouse during the summer and rewarded those who stayed in the winter with life affirming warmth.

Lucky walked down past the boardwalk, past the wharf, to the point where the land jetted out into the water. A peaceful and serene place, with no traffic. The road had been blocked off to make way for a pedestrian and bike path. A few benches lined the edge near the cliff. A person had to be careful, if he wasn't paying attention. It was a long way down. Surfers would climb down the hill, scrambling down rocky pathways, to get to the beach and their domain.

On a bench overlooking the water, Lucky and Heather sometimes sat and watched the surfers. Other times, if the water was calm and glassy, and there were no surfers around, they'd sit on a bench and hold hands, waiting for the sun to go down.

Today, he sat on a bench, and Winslow jumped up next to him. He eavesdropped on a couple of men standing nearby. Surfers who stood near the edge of the cliff, looking down at the water, shaking their heads.

"Not too good."

"There's a swell coming in from the northwest."

Lucky didn't know anything about a swell, but he knew there were always surfers coming and going, from before sunrise to dusk. They sounded like weather experts, talking about swells, tides, the moon, direction of the wind. He heard them debating which Internet sites had the best Web cams on the surf.

He couldn't relate to their patience, sitting out in the water on their boards for hours, waiting for what, he didn't know. They'd be covered head to toe in black wetsuits. Even their feet were covered with matching slipper-like rubber socks. The wetsuits, Heather had told him, were necessary unless they wanted to suffer from hypothermia, the water being colder than it seemed.

Lucky just thought the surfers looked as if they were in

some private club, and their wet suits were a uniform that bound them together in some mysterious way.

"Let's check it out," the younger guy with the bleached hair said to the other. The older guy had shoulder length, salt and pepper hair, tied back into a ponytail.

The two men stood at the edge of the cliff, looking down at the water with surfboards in hand, dissecting its every nuance and surveying their kingdom. "You ride goofy-foot, don't you?"

"Yup, whether I want to or not," the teen said, zipping up the back of his suit. "Let's go."

"I'm ready."

"How's your IPO going?" The elder asked. He had taken the young guy under his wing since he was the grand-father of the waves, being over forty, and his protégé still in his teens.

"It's in the pipeline."

They laughed and headed down the cliff to the water.

Lucky watched as the two traversed down the steep, rocky embankment following a narrow, pathway, balancing their surfboards as if they were walking a high wire act at the circus. Lucky didn't know how they managed to get down without falling on their asses.

Before they entered the water, the surfers stopped to wrap a Velcro strip around their ankles, which was attached to a leash connected to their board. Then they paddled out, each finding their space on the waves, their own freedom in a busy world, it seemed.

Lucky decided to descend the cliff. "Come on, boy," he said, taking the leash off of the dog. Winslow was already down the cliff and waiting for Lucky who was taking his shoes off, figuring it was easier barefoot. He left his shoes on the bench and climbed down.

"Go get it, boy," Lucky said, as he took the fuzzy tennis ball out of his sweatshirt pocket. He threw the ball as far as possible into the water, causing one of the surfers who'd been paddling out to turn around.

"Watch out, asshole."

"Sorry," Lucky said. No, he wasn't.

Winslow retrieved the ball, and Lucky threw it back out again, this time missing the surfer, even though he aimed for him. Lucky stood on the edge of the water where the sand changed color from salt to pepper. The water dampened the sand as it lapped over his bare feet.

"You'll never amount to nothin', you bum."

Lucky turned around suddenly.

"Got the devil in yuh, kid. Always will."

"Shut up," Lucky said. Looking around, he saw no one. He heard only his father's voice. Would it ever leave him for good? Maybe if he hadn't killed him and froze the image in his mind, they wouldn't keep haunting him. He could see him lying on the hard floor in a pool of his own blood, his angry fists gone limp. His black and angry eyes, vacant. The anxiety inside of Lucky filled him like a balloon with too much helium. He'd be dammed if some goofy-footed surfer hit it big before he did.

Lucky pried the heavily soaked ball from Winslow's jaw, then threw it back to sea, where it disappeared in the undertow. He wished he could throw away the wicked memories so easily.

The thought of not proceeding with his life left him as stagnant as the opaque lagoon that ran alongside the far side of the wharf, an area the tourists never saw.

And, his feelings for Heather were getting too intense.

Lucky needed to have a better agenda than spending his days waiting on people who didn't look at the entree price. His evenings were spent with a girl who sat on his lap reading a textbook, while an anxious dog waited by the door with a ball in his mouth asking for his daily walk to the beach, watching surfers catch waves and talk about their windfalls.

The words the seamen left him with were distant memories. He'd almost forgotten their advice. Work hard. You'll get rewarded. Instead, he only heard his father's voice. You'll never amount to nothin'.

"Come on, boy, let's go back to the house," Lucky said, climbing back up the cliff.

The windows were steamed, and the scent of garlic bread filled the air.

"Can I borrow your car tomorrow?" Lucky asked.

"Sure, honey," she agreed, leaning over to kiss him on his tanned cheek, right below the scar under his eye. She placed the last item on the table, completing the meal, a breadbasket rested next to a vase holding pink lilies and baby's breath.

Heather had already decided that tomorrow night she was going to tell him her secret. She'd splurge her tip money, and make a special dinner of baked salmon with shallots and rice pudding for dessert. Her life couldn't be more perfect. Her parents were wrong. She could live on her own, be self-sufficient, and be quite happy. Plus, she'd found the love of her life. The news she had for Lucky would make their lives complete.

"Since I have the lunch shift, I'll bring it back to you at Chez Von."

"What?" She wasn't paying attention. She was too busy thinking about tomorrow night.

"Dinner ready yet?" Lucky asked.

"Yes, it is."

Excellent. Dinner was ready. Pasta, green salad, and seasoned bread. What more could he ask for? Maybe an IPO in the pipeline.

*   *   *

Chez Von overlooked the southern edge of San Francisco Bay, and was perched on a hill, hidden in soaring eucalyptus trees off the mountainous scenic Highway 280. Lucky heard the road was called the most beautiful highway in the world by some. The exclusive restaurant was a discreet place for the executives of Silicon Valley to meet and exchange secrets. This was where deals, business and otherwise, were consummated.

His job enabled Lucky to eavesdrop on privileged conversations. An insight into the high-powered valley elite who saw themselves as being above everyone else because of the cars they drove and the seemingly endless supply of money they had at their disposal.

Lucky wanted it, all of it.

Heather had taken the bus when he'd borrowed her car. He told her that he had to see someone about the paperwork needed to stay in the country legally. In reality, he just wanted to drive around and think, never having made an appointment with an attorney.

He placed his work uniform of black pants and white long-sleeved dress shirt flat on the back seat, put the convertible top down, and turned the radio to a jazz station. He drove north through San Francisco and over the Golden Gate Bridge. A carload of women passed him in the slow traffic. They smiled and waved at him. He knew women were attracted to him. He was hot, and he knew it.

Waving back to the women, he considered driving farther than he already had, following the highway that hugged the coastline leading all the way into Oregon, a state he had not yet explored. But, he changed his mind when he realized the gas gauge was nearing empty. Even a Volkswagen needed gas on occasion. After passing the marina village of Sausalito, he made a U-turn and drove back over the bridge.

Pulling into the Chez Von parking lot, he saw a white Rolls-Royce pull out. Doing a double take, he saw a chauffeur in a dark-colored cap. In the back seat was a man with silver hair. As the car left the lot, Lucky read the license plate, "SANGER1."

Ignoring the sign that read, "Patron Parking Only," Lucky pulled into a space between a BMW and a Jaguar.

Why should he be relegated to the employee lot behind the building?

Getting out, he changed into his work uniform, not caring if anyone saw him. Finger-combing his hair on his way inside, he wondered what kind of a day today would be.

*   *   *

Lucky spotted forty-ish Jennifer Jones, or J.J., just as soon as he walked into the restaurant. She wasn't hard to notice, being a high-powered, high-profiled Silicon Valley woman whom he'd seen and read about in Technology Today, the daily Silicon Valley Bible.

The paper needed to get a new photographer. The black and white photos hadn't done justice to her shoulder length, shiny black hair, curled slightly at the ends. And money-green eyes that reflected big bucks. Her sleeveless dress was more appropriate for a summer wedding than a business lunch. Talk about cleavage, hers barely fit the low-cut v-neckline. She was all woman, not like skinny Heather and most of the other girls on the beach. Peeking out under the fine linen tablecloth, he could see high-heeled bone-colored shoes, legs unburdened by nylons.

"I conferenced with Barney and John Dunn."

"Barney?" J.J. asked, not paying attention.

"The investment banker," Gloria said, disgusted that J.J. wasn't listening.

"Right, of course, sorry. I was just zoning," J.J. said, wondering how high the stock would go on its first day of trading.

"From what I hear, you're all set for the twenty-third. There's nothing else big that day. You'll explode the market," Gloria said.

J.J. liked the idea that Gloria was an attorney specializing in the complicated high-tech ring, and she was a friend whom she could trust implicitly.

*   *   *

"You're late." Heather said, looking upset.

"I was busy," he said, rolling his eyes.

"Did you go see the attorney?" she asked nervously.

"What are you, my mother?" Lucky asked, immediately regretting his harsh tone. His heart ached because he didn't know what it felt like to have a mother.

Heather's eyes welled up. After all, she was trying to be nice. Her boyfriend could snap at a moment's notice.

Lucky ignored her, turning his attention to Robbie Barnes. Why did Heather need this Robbie character, anyway? That was beyond Lucky's comprehension.

Heather said something, but her words went over Lucky's head. Instead, he zoomed his eyes in on the over-bleached, too-short-haired, bony six-foot-one Robbie. When the bum wasn't waiting tables, he tried to establish himself as a singer, model, actor, or something equally stupid. The guy had what he wanted. Table Six. The most requested seating at Chez Von.

The tales of Silicon Valley success that transpired over three-hour lunches at Chez Von were endless. However, what transactions took place at Table Six were beyond calculation. Lucky had read in the trades Table Six was where Billy Sanger was sitting when he closed many deals to earn his billionaire status.

Sanger Systems became one of the world's most successful software firms, and Billy Sanger one of the world's richest men. He kept himself scarce in the public eye, preferring to stay inside his mansion down the peninsula in ultra-exclusive Atherton where the residents needed a net of at least a billion just to buy property there.

Lucky wanted to be Billy Sanger.

The roundtable was tucked into the corner of the

restaurant with unparalleled views of the valley and beyond, all the way to the ocean where high-powered Silicon Valleyites sat and discussed their next power play. Everyone wanted this table. The table of success.

Lucky followed Robbie into the kitchen.

"I'll take over Table Six."

"Forget it," Robbie said. He was sick of Lucky trying to play boss. This was a matter of seniority. Lucky has kicked him and the other waiters around long enough. Who did he think he was, the owner of Chez Von?

"Here's a smoke. Go take a break," Lucky said, handing Robbie a single cigarette from the front pocket of his shirt.

"I don't smoke," Robbie said, disgusted at the very idea of it. He wouldn't do anything that could lead to the destruction of what he'd spent years honing, his sun avoided skin, heart, his lungs. After singing in the San Francisco Gay Men's Chorus, his lungs were strong and good, just as they would remain.

"Well, you should start," Lucky said, putting the cigarette in Robbie's shirt pocket. "It'll transform you into a man."

"I am a man." Robbie's eyes narrowed. He tore the filterless cigarette into two pieces and tossed it to the ground.

"Right," Lucky said, giving a sarcastic air.

"What did you say?"

"Don't get in a tizzy," Lucky pushed him aside.

"You asshole."

"Oh, Lover Boy can swear. You been sneaking in the wine cellar again?"

"You-son-of-a-bitch. I'll get you."

"Are you threatening me?" Laughing, Lucky couldn't stop himself. "And just what are you going to do? Tell your mommy?" Why did he say that? He always went too far.

"Just wait." Robbie restrained himself from hitting him, his back stiffened in spasms. He decided to leave the juvenile and left the kitchen for the foyer to bring Jean-Marc, the manager in to resolve the dispute.

Lucky glanced over and saw Robbie and Jean-Marc huddled in a corner. Deep in conversation. Trying his best to ignore them, he headed straight for his prey, the high-tech power ladies at Table Six.

*   *   *

"I really need to talk to you," Heather said, just as he was about to descend on the table.

"Not now, Heather," he whispered. Not in this restaurant that was his meal ticket to schmoozing the rich and famous into noticing him. "Soon, Heather, I promise."

Walking away, he didn't notice the longing in her eyes, or her love for a man who was too preoccupied to notice, or care.

*   *   *

"What do you think you're doing?" Jean-Marc asked, grabbing Lucky's arm, pinching it until it throbbed.

"Working. What does it look like?" He yanked his arm away, pissed.

"Follow me into the kitchen."

Lucky was steamed, but followed Jean-Marc.

The second the door shut behind them, Jean-Marc let him have it. "Where do you get off causing me trouble with my employee? Don't push, young man, or you're aiming for a harassment suit."

"For what?" Lucky shook his head. "Making a pass at him? The guy's paranoid."

"What were you doing at his table? Table Six isn't your responsibility."

"Robbie walked away, and the women appeared to need attention. Is it my fault he neglected his duties? I pay attention to my tables. Why do you think I get the biggest tips in this joint?" There wasn't a doubt that he was the best waiter they had, and Jean-Marc would be hard pressed to find reason to fire him.

"Well, just stay cool, and watch your attitude, pal, or you're out of here. Got it?" Had Jean-Marc fallen into Lucky's charm trap?

"Tell you what," Lucky said, ignoring the out-of-here comment. "I'll take Table Five, if you assign me Six."

Jean-Marc looked out at Five. A traveling businessman who probably didn't speak English. He knew that the other waiters never wanted to take the time to translate the menu. There were enough complaints, especially from Robbie who hated translating. Lucky didn't know Japanese any more than the next guy, but he had a way with foreign customers as he had with locals.

"Get busy, then," Jean-Marc said, rubbing the smooth, therapeutic worry stones in his pocket. He knew he'd have to smooth things over with Robbie, somehow.

*   *   *

"Can I take your order?" Lucky asked the man at Table Five.

The Japanese businessman, wearing a permanent smile, set the menu down on the table and readied to try his English. He read and understood more English than he let on. The restaurant wasn't as expensive as he thought. Triple-digit lunches. He was used to paying as much in Tokyo.

"Yes, tank you."

"Ready to order, sir?" he repeated.

"Yes, tank you."

Lucky rolled his eyes. Ever since a Kobe, Japan Web site for Bay Area bound travelers reviewed Chez Von as being the place to see and be seen, they had been inundated with eager Japanese taste buds.

The man pointed to a lobster being carried past the table

on a tray.

"I understand, I'll be right out with your lobster," Lucky said, moving on to Table Six.

"How is everything?" he asked, winking at the one in the high-heels.

The women were already on their second or third drinks and were working on salads with a fancy French name, enabling the restaurant to charge more for just green lettuce and trimmings.

Feeling Lucky's masculine presence, J.J. didn't look up, trying to not think about sex. Instead, she wanted to keep focused on business, which she was having enough trouble doing. "Everything is fine," she said, taking a bite of romaine lettuce with blue cheese.

"If there's anything I can get you, just let me know," Lucky said. He went to smooth things over with Heather.

*   *   *

"You didn't have to get so grouchy," she said, rubbing her eyes as if she'd been tired.

"Sorry, babe." He gazed back over to the women. They were engrossed in conversation. Probably talking about some big Silicon Valley deal that was going to make them millions. More than they already had.

*   *   *

"That waiter is Brad Pitt gorgeous," Gloria said, sucking the pimento out the center of the martini olive.

"Which waiter?" J.J. asked. Her heels were killing her. She couldn't wait to get home and take them off after her appointment.

"Our new one. Didn't you see the way he drooled over you?" Ignoring her napkin, Gloria wiped away the juice from the olive that had dribbled down her chin with the back of her hand. Feeling tipsy, she wondered if the last martini was one too many.

"You have a vivid imagination," J.J. said. She looked over at the waiter who was talking to the hostess with the sun-bleached blonde hair and flat chest. "Besides he looks more like Josh Hartnett."

*   *   *

"Did you look over the brochures?" Heather asked Lucky softly, almost in a whisper.

"Uh—I told you. No money for that."

He was acutely aware that the two women at Six were staring at him. They wore seductive smiles that spoke his language. The sexual language.

"Scholarships are available. I can talk to my counselor," Heather said, almost desperate, but Lucky was not paying much attention.

*   *   *

"He's young enough to be your summer intern," J.J. said, pushing her half-eaten salad aside.

She was hungry, but didn't feel like eating. Glancing over at him, she noticed Lucky's tight, black uniform pants, accentuating the bulge in front. The crisp white, oxford, button-down shirt contrasted well with his jet-black hair, matching the unusual dark color of his mysterious eyes. He was tan, firm, young and had the body that made women melt at first glance.

"Oh, I hadn't noticed him," J.J. lied. "Now, can we get back to business, please?"

*   *   *

"We'll talk about this later," Lucky said to Heather, in an angry tone.

He returned to the kitchen and came out carrying lobster and green tea for the still-smiling Japanese businessman, who nodded in thanks.

Returning to Table Six, with a stomach that felt as if he'd swallowed a paperweight, Lucky wondered if his turn in the fast lane would ever come. Would the man with the checkered flag ever wave him in?

*   *   *

"How was everything?" he asked the redhead.

"Just fine," Gloria said, putting down her Gucci lipstick mirror on the table. "By the way, what's your name?"

"Lucky."

"Are you?" she asked, tilting her head, hoping he would wink at her this time.

"I'm lucky to be servicing you two beautiful ladies."

"You mean serving," J.J. corrected, pointing to her plate.

"Oh, right," he said, smiling at her, removing her plate from the table.

J.J. rolled her eyes. "We'll have two coffees please. Black."

*   *   *

"Still got a job, asshole?" Robbie asked as Lucky reached for the coffee pot.

"Of course, I do." Lucky sounded as sweet as possible, then walked away. He didn't want to talk to the bum. Not now. The jerk's attitude was sickening. Lucky liked nothing about the guy, not his lifestyle choices or his bleached hair, compliments of Heather who had gone to his house in the city one Saturday to bleach it.

Putting Robbie out of his mind, Lucky balanced the steaming cups on a heavy, genuine silver tray. As he approached the women's table from behind, he slowed down and listened without their knowledge, to their ping-pong conversation.

"Buy JBC now."

"I need a good orgasm."

"They are going to announce a re-org."

"I can't find a good assistant."

"Their burn rate is five million a month."

"Don't tell anyone, but—"

Lucky heard enough. His moment had come. Quickly, he assessed the situation. She needed an assistant. Great. He had a viable in.

"Here's your coffee. Would you ladies like anything else?" He wanted to make his move, but not there in the restaurant. Outside, maybe.

"Just the bill," J.J. said.

"Right, I'll be right back," he said, then went to calculate their total.

Turning to Gloria, J.J. said, "I have an appointment."

"Right. The shrink."

"She's not a shrink."

"Sorry. Therapist." Gloria reached into her tweed Kate Spade purse for the hundred-dollar bill that she kept safely inside a zipped pocket. She was an all-cash girl. No credit cards for her. Not since her ex-husband destroyed her credit rating.

Lucky came back with the bill. Laying the leather billfold holding the lunch tab on the table, he noticed a set of keys. They were attached to a small, half-dollar-sized piece of bronze metal. On it was engraved, Santa Ri . . . something. He couldn't read the whole thing, a lipstick-smeared napkin covered the rest. What was it with American women and their lipstick?

"Here you go," Gloria said, handing him the cash. Enough for the salads, drinks and a worthwhile tip for the lad, even if he didn't wink at her.

While Gloria stumbled out of the restaurant, J.J. went to

the ladies room.

Gloria loved the peppermint scent of the massive euca-lyptus trees and savored the short walk out to the parking lot. The autumn sun was warm, balmy. Electricity filled the air, a few ominous clouds hung over the mountains, and she feared an earthquake, but her Harvard trained mind told her that predicting an earthquake based on weather was a categorical impossibility. But still, after work, when she got home in the city, she made a mental note to double-check her emergency earthquake supply kit, filled with canned food, water and a first aid kit, just to be safe.

Gloria wasn't looking forward to driving back into the city. This was as close as she ever got to being in the country, distancing herself from the constant demand for problem solving that she called work.

*   *   *

Lucky looked around the restaurant. The high-powered lunch crowd was weeding out. Everyone had to get back to their mergers and stock options, he assumed. Every busi-nessperson must have thought theirs was the next pioneering solution. They most likely were convinced that they would become the next Billy Sanger.

Heather was looking at the college brochures that Lucky wanted no part of. Jean-Marc was on the phone. Robbie was waiting on Table Fourteen. The Japanese businessman was sipping the last of his green tea.

Lucky slipped the keys into his pocket.

J.J. found Gloria already outside about to get into her sports car. Both women liked their martinis equally as much.

"You okay to drive?"

"I'm fine. Don't worry about me," Gloria said.

"Earthquake weather, huh?" J.J. said, looking up at the sky.

"There's no such thing."

"Sorry, I forgot, you haven't experienced a big one yet."

"Oh, I've had my share of big ones."

They both laughed.

"Be careful driving, dear, and I'll see you soon," J.J. said, blowing her a kiss. She admired the way Gloria had picked up her life following the divorce from the asshole who had taken to visiting a certain massage parlor he'd discovered on the Internet.

Massages only, he tried to convince Gloria once she discovered the charges to the Visa bill and began to investigate. She turned him and the house of prostitution over to the police. When the vice squad raided the joint, the owner cried foul, saying it was a free country, and he thought that meant he could do what he wanted, even if it involved underage females.

"Bye, sweetie," Gloria said, getting into her sports car. She sped away, at first driving on the wrong side of the road, but correcting herself when she realized a car was headed straight for her.

J.J. stood next to her Mercedes-Benz, rummaging through her purse. "Crap," she said. "Where are my Goddamn keys?"

Lucky patted the keys in his pocket. "I'm taking a break," he said to Jean-Marc, who was on the phone scheduling a reservation.

Jean-Marc's real name was John Martin, but at the restaurant, he assumed another character. And, when he added a fake French accent, his tips doubled. Being recently made into acting manager only increased his sense of authority. Jean-Marc held the phone to his chest. "You just got here. No break."

"Who does that guy think he is?" Jean-Marc asked Heather, who stood beside him at the hostess stand.

Heather had stuffed the college brochures into her 500-page Shakespeare book that needed finishing by the next day. She would make sure Lucky read them when he returned.

"Where are you going?" asked Heather, as Lucky headed out the front door.

He didn't have time to stop and talk now. Enough time had been wasted. The keys to their future were in his pocket and time was of the essence.

She suddenly felt as if she had drunk a glass of buttermilk. Her stomach churned. What was on Lucky's mind?

"To join the fast lane." No looking back now.

She worried about him. He'd seemed edgy for a while, reading all those business magazines. She told him that if he was interested in business, he should enroll in college. The informational brochures had been in the duplex living room for weeks, laying on the plastic upside down milk crate they used for a coffee table. He never even picked them up. She was sure he saw them; after all, she'd pointed them out enough times. Maybe she hadn't been forceful enough.

Heather went back to checking the reservation list. She planned to ask him about enrolling in college later. After work. After she read her homework assignment. After she threw up.

*   *   *

'Lucky followed the woman in the heels out to her car. "Excuse me, ma'am."

J.J. looked toward him. "What?" What could the waiter want? The last thing she needed was a testosterone trophy, or maybe it was exactly what she needed. A quick orgasm in the back seat of her car, then back to work.

In vain, she kept searching for her car keys. If she had to call the towing service, she'd show up late for an appointment with Dr. Wells. The good doctor was a shrink, her shrink. She just didn't want to be late for her forty-five minute treatment now that she thought she was making progress. Plus, her sanity needed calming, and Dr. Wells wouldn't authorize any more Xanax without her coming into the office. The pills were like being on vacation, and she needed a vacation real bad.

"Excuse me, ma'am, I think you need these." Lucky seductively dangled the car keys in front of her, stopping just short of her full breasts.

Trying not to look at him, she grabbed the keys from his hand, pressed the lock release, and got in the car. She started the car, but could feel his presence as if he were inside with her.

"I have a proposition for you," he said over the engine vibrations.

J.J. turned the volume of the stereo up so she could better enjoy the sound, but she enjoyed men even more. She put the car in reverse, backed out, and headed out of the parking lot. Soon, she would be at Dr. Wells' office, trying to find the underlying cause of her problems. She had everything, yet she had nothing at all.

As J.J. drove away, she looked back, noticing the waiter was still standing there. He had charm and looks that were undeniably irresistible. As she drove past him, she took another glimpse. He was young. Too young. Was he expecting a reward? "Dammit." She made a quick U-turn, causing the driver of the car behind her to honk his horn. Road rage. Just what she needed.

"Up yours," she said as the car flew passed her, the driver gave her the finger. She didn't care. There was something about the waiter she couldn't resist. She wanted him. Dr. Wells wouldn't mind if she were a few minutes late for the weekly analysis. After all, the good doctor had made enough money off her, and now she would take just a minute to thank the young man.

Lucky flashed a smile as she opened the window. Was this the window of his new life?

Jennifer Jones didn't know if it was the martinis talking, but he was too gorgeous to let slip away. He was magnetic and his charm, inescapable. Dr. Wells could wait. Her newfound treasure could not.

Chapter Five

J.J.'s longing between her legs twitched in anticipation. "Here's ten dollars. Thanks for finding my keys."

"Just part of my job," Lucky said, stuffing it into his pants pocket. Ten bucks was ten bucks.

"Well . . . well, I have to get going," she said, starting to feel sixteen again. Stuttering and not knowing what to say next wasn't in her character. She was always in control.

"Listen," Lucky said, unwilling to let this moment slip like the San Andreas Fault. "I couldn't help but overhear your conversation—"

Oh, shit, J.J. thought. This guy was going to blackmail her. He must have heard Gloria giving her inside trader information. And she thought he was a young greenhorn, someone just off the boat. Someone she could play with in the afternoons and screw her brains out when the mood struck. J.J. shook her head. "I really have to go, there's an appointment that I'm already late for." Reaching into her briefcase, she pulled out a business card. "Call me and we can work out a deal."

Lucky read the card, misinterpreting what she'd meant. "Miss Jones, I would love to work for you. What an honor to learn from the best."

"Work for me? But, I thought—"

"I heard you say you needed a new assistant, and I would like to offer my services." Lucky extended his hand.

"By the way, Ms. Jones, my real name is Lane." Hesitating, he felt his cheeks turn red. "Lawson, Lane Lawson." Just like that, Lucky Lukovich was gone, in his place a new person. A person born to rule Silicon Valley. The next time the newborn Lane Lawson would go to Chez Von would be as a paying customer.

Relieved, J.J. laughed at herself for thinking he was a

blackmailer. All he wanted was a job. Was she becoming paranoid? She had to convince the pharmacist to refill her prescription. She missed her appointment with Dr. Wells, but she found a new assistant. Not a bad trade off. Besides, with the company going public any minute, she could use all the help in the office and all the stress relief at home that she could muster.

"So, where do you live?" she asked.

"Over the hill. Been sharing a place."

"If you need a place to live—"

"No, I—"

"Besides, over the hill won't do. I need any assistant of mine to be close by. Hours will be long and the work treacherous."

He hadn't planned on moving out on Heather.

"If you want to make it in this business, you'd be wise to listen to me."

"Oh?" He wanted to be successful, so he and Heather could live in style one day soon.

"I can put you up for a while." She smiled at the thought.

"Well . . ."

"Hop in. You can start right away."

Lucky glanced back at Chez Von. How could he just walk out on Heather? She'd wanted to talk to him. But, this was for Heather as much as for himself.

"Great," he said, getting into the car. They drove over the hill to the beach, a twenty-minute drive.

"You can get your stuff," she said.

Traffic was light; it was too early for the afternoon rush. Silicon Valley exodus started about four. The departure included surfer wanna-be Silicon Valley executives who tried in vain to be cool by living in beach front condos bought with stock options that skyrocketed on their first day of trading. As she maneuvered the curves of the mountainous road like a pro, she informed him of the terms of their employer-employee relationship.

He agreed, with little apprehension. Executive Assistant to Jennifer Jones, President of Nomadic Software. He'd get a decent salary, benefits, and, as she had said, if he played his cards right, the golden egg of them all, stock options. Not bad for a guy not long off the boat.

They soon arrived at the duplex. J.J. waited in the car as he went after his meager belongings.

Lucky took the extra key from under the geranium pot, as he hadn't had his key with him. The dog greeted him with a wagging tail when he went in. Petting him on the head, Lucky went into the bedroom, with the dog following closely behind.

He took his backpack out of the closet, and filled it with some clothes. He could always get the rest another time. In the dresser drawer, he removed his mother's picture, and the dried gardenia that he'd kept since that first day when he met Heather. The gardenia blossom was crumbling. Like he didn't want his life to be. He had the urge to throw it away, but instead took an envelope out of Heather's desk drawer and gently placed the dead bloom in it before putting in his backpack. He folded the picture of his mother and placed it in his wallet.

Glancing over at a framed picture on the nightstand, he sat down on the bed and held it in his unsteady hand. He knew it had been there, yet never noticed it before. It was a grainy color photo of himself and Heather. He remembered the night that they had posed for it. The boardwalk was dark and misty. An unusual night because it hadn't been too crowded. They had shared a crab cocktail on the wharf and then walked hand in hand for hours. First along the pier, then along the nearby shore, then around the boardwalk, where the colorfully lit rides seemed to sing a song just for the two of them.

Later, she talked him into squeezing into a booth, and they spent their last few dollars on silly photos. That was where they had kissed for the first time.

He put the photo back on the table. "Am I doing the right thing?" he asked Winslow. Lucky decided now was not the time to be sentimental. He went into the kitchen to look for some money.

"Jackpot," he said, looking in a tea tin in the cupboard behind a box of granola. Helping himself to three hundred dollars, he felt like a thief, and the dog was the witness. "This is my tip money too, you know."

Lucky looked around the kitchen. Dirty dishes were stacked in the sink. Bananas in the fruit bowl on the counter were speckled with black dots.

On the floor, he noticed the dog's two dishes. Instinctively, he leaned down and picked up Winslow's water dish and dumped out the stale water to fill it with fresh. "Here you go, boy." He poured some dry dog food into his other bowl.

On his way out of the kitchen, he took a pink lily out of the vase on the table. Of course, the flowers had been from Robbie.

The dog followed his master to the front door. He seemed to know.

"I'm sorry, buddy."

Winslow's eyes drooped, as if he was losing his best pal.

Outside, the engine was running as J.J. waited. She noticed that a bird had just relieved itself on her windshield. "Dammit." Looking up, she noticed a street sign that read, NUCLEAR FREE ZONE. As she shook her head, she heard loud music approaching from the rear of the car. She hit the button locking all the doors.

A flurry of purple hair walked by. Teens wearing fluo-rescent-colored tie-dyed T-shirts and baggy-to-the-extreme jeans. The tall, skinny one had a boom box rest-ing on his shoulder. The shorter, plumper guy bopped like a rooster. Did they think they were at a costume party or a dance contest? Laughing, J.J. was sure the event would be for the culturally challenged.

"Car's locked," Lucky said, knocking on the passenger side window, unfazed by the kids walking by.

"Sorry. There you go," she said, popping open the electric lock.

"Here, this is for you." He handed her the flower.

"That's so sweet of you." She tossed it into the back seat. She couldn't wait to get back over the hill, to her side of the valley. To civilization.

"This is a great set of wheels," he said, throwing the sack filled with all his early belongings into the back seat of the Mercedes, as he got in. His butt fit firmly into the leather passenger seat. A smile crossed his lips. Good fortune was his for the taking.

"Can I borrow your cell phone for a second? I gotta make a call."

"If you don't have your own cell, first thing we'll do is get you one."

"That'd be great."

"Go ahead, and take my phone out of my purse," she said.

He dialed the number he knew by heart.

"Chez Von."

He recognized Jean-Marc's voice. He expected Heather to answer the phone. "Lucky here. Put Heather on. Oh, and by the way, I quit. I won't be in any more except to pick up my last paycheck."

"Dammit, Lucky. You can't quit without notice," Jean-Marc said, although he was glad to be rid of him. "But if you are quitting, I'm deducting those calls to New York."

"I told you, I never called New York," Lucky lied. So what if he called once or twice to check on Dina? He had to call several times to get information about her progress. "Just get Heather." There was no time for Jean-Marc's sniveling.

"Lucky?" She heard the conversation with Jean-Marc and knew what was coming; knew before he had even said a word. She'd seen how he looked running out of the restaurant—out of her life—into his own.

"Heather, try not to cry," he said, anticipating her tears.

"Who was the whore in the Mercedes?" Heather asked. "Jean-Marc saw you getting into her car."

"Calm down."

"How long has this been–"

A customer tapping her fingernails on the reservation podium, interrupted Heather. "Excuse me, I have a reservation. Mrs. Dunn."

Sasha Dunn was not one to be kept waiting. She learned from her husband to command power, but often found that when she was out in public without him, people didn't respect her. She suspected their rudeness was because of her skin tone, her mother being Swedish and her father African-American. But, when she was on the arm of her husband, it was a different story, then people couldn't do enough for her.

"Just a minute," Heather said, not looking up.

Blowing the wisps of her frizzy, honey-colored hair off her forehead, Sasha was sure that if the girl saw who she was, it would make a difference.

"Is there a problem?" Brianna Montgomery, Sasha's lunch companion, asked loudly.

"Not at all," Sasha said. How she hated Brianna, but if she could get her vote for the position of Chairman of the Winter Ball, then the coveted spot would be hers. The others of the committee would follow Brianna's lead.

Heather's hand trembled while she listened to Lucky talk. She felt as if she had gone deep sea diving without an air tank. Feeling faint, she leaned on the podium, resting against the solid oak, her only support.

"I'm doing this for us," Lucky said, glancing over at J.J. whose hands clutched firmly on the steering wheel. A diamond bracelet dangled from one wrist, a Rolex watch on the other.

J.J. looked over, and he smiled at her. She was his new money machine.

Lucky's words only made Heather more upset. She had taken him in, giving him a place to live when he was homeless. She found him a job. He used her car. So, what had he done? Leave her? For who, some libertine in an expensive car?

Eavesdropping, her specialty, Sasha softened, feeling sorry for the young girl who obviously wasn't as experienced with men as herself. Leaning toward the girl whose tanned face had lost its color, she offered advice. "Don't let him talk to you that way. You be strong, girl. Tell him where he can go."

Heather straightened her slumping self and mouthed thank you to the lady she now recognized as Mrs. Dunn.

"Lucky, if you were really thinking of us—you'd be here. Go if you must, but you'll live to regret it." She slammed the phone down, causing the reservation list to tumble to the floor in her breeze.

"You go, girl," Sasha said, glad that the attention would now turn to her. Her table awaited her presence. Smoothing out her Victor Costa suit, she nodded to Brianna. She was capable of handling this, and she was capable of handling the Annual Winter Ball.

"You, okay?" Robbie asked. He'd been watching from a distance, and knew if Lucky was involved, there would be trouble. He put his arm around her, giving her a compassionate hug. "It'll be all right." He loved his friend and there wasn't anything he wouldn't do for her.

"Robbie?"

"What, Heather?" He gently wiped a warm tear from her soft cheek.

"I don't feel so good. Can you show Mrs. Dunn and her guest to their table?" Heather ran to the bathroom.

*   *   *

Lucky was somewhat nervous with his new benefactor. "Got that squared away."

"I'm glad," she said, glancing over. He'd removed his

shirt, leaving on only a white T-shirt. She noticed a heart-shaped tattoo on his arm. The body art turned her on even more. He was a bad boy, too. What a bonus.

She confidently placed her hand on his thigh. "You've made the right decision." He was gorgeous, sexy and just what the doctor ordered. "I'll take you right to my place, so you can settle in."

Lucky squirmed as a city bus passed them with several passengers gawking out the window at them. He felt as if they knew what he'd done and realized how bad a bad person he was. Had they known J.J. was trying to unzip his pants as they drove down the freeway? What had he gotten himself into?

"Maybe later," he said, brushing J.J.'s hand away. He felt guilty with the erection coming on, but if this was what she wanted, so be it. This was what it would take. End of story.

When they arrived, he ran through the condo, which boasted a million-dollar view of the bay. This was a present with his name on it. This would do just fine. "How long have yuh lived here?" he asked, trying to stifle a sneeze.

J.J. was mixing a screwdriver. "Couple of years. I gotta call the office. Make yourself at home." She took off her heels and threw them on the raspberry-colored silk damask sofa that her longhaired cat kept covered with white fur.

"Your cat, no good," Quintina, the maid, often said in disgust, having to hand pick the cat's long, white fur off the furniture. But, that was Quintina's job, to keep the furniture clean along with the rest of the elegant residence.

Lucky helped himself to some leftover Chinese food and a Heineken. The kitchen was done in all black. Black walls. Black sink. The only thing that wasn't black was the counter top and it was concrete. Very strange, he thought. California was odd.

With his food and a beer, he went into the living room. The wall of windows looked out onto a redwood-filled mountain that seemed almost close enough to touch. The other wall was filled with photos, reading like a "Who's Who of Silicon Valley." Photos of J.J. with all the people Lucky had been reading about. Studying. Ready to take on.

Underneath the photo display was a fish tank he guessed to be holding at least fifty gallons of water. Fluorescent-colored fish swam in never-ending circles.

Where's the TV? He set the beer bottle, now half-empty, and container of cold chow mein on a glass coffee table.

"Couldn't find the remote. Actually, can't find the TV," he said as he sauntered down the hallway looking for J.J. Standing in the doorway of her study, he could see out the window. Nothing but blue sky and gray water filled with boats, probably headed for Pac Bell Park. He'd read about a ball game that was scheduled later tonight. He surmised that the boats would jockey for position to catch fly balls. Couldn't they find anything better to do?

"I'm working," she said. "Go watch TV."

"That's just—"

J.J. got up from her desk and shut the door before he could finish his sentence. If he was going to live with her, he needed to be aware of his boundaries. This room was off limits.

Returning to her ergonomically correct chair, she aligned the basket of pens and calculator on top of the desk with the natural wood lines. Dr. Wells said she had a tendency to be compulsive, but she didn't think so. What had it mattered if she grabbed an anti-bacterial tissue and wiped the phone receiver before making a call?

Lucky listened outside the door. She didn't have to be a bitch to him.

"Sorry 'bout that—had a flat tire—need to reschedule."

Lucky decided it wasn't anything too interesting and went to unpack his few belongings. He made himself at home in the master bedroom suite. The opulent bedroom alone was larger than the ground floor duplex he had shared with Heather. Not bad, he thought, putting his clothes into a bureau drawer next to her one-piece bathing suits.

Looking over at the circular-shaped bed that was positioned in the center of the room, he thought he had seen it in a magazine spread on the Valley's wealthy. And, just like in the magazine, her longhaired white cat was asleep on the center of the bed amid dozens of throw pillows. The ceiling mirror above the bed hadn't shown up in the photo layout, though.

After taking a shower, much like being under a warm cascading waterfall, he wrapped a fluffy, king-sized towel around his waist and sat on the enormous bed.

Sneezing three times in a row, he went back to the bathroom and got a box of tissue from what looked like the cosmetics counter at Macy's. He had gone there once with Heather and her tip money.

Out through the French doors he went. The private terrace was inviting, so he grabbed his cigarettes, lighter and nose tissues. A quarter-moon lit the surroundings just enough to not have to turn on the outdoor lights. Flowerpots filled with sweet-smelling blooms graced the terrace. On one end of the patio, he noticed a marble statue of a naked man. On the other end was a bar-b-que that looked like it had never been used. He looked forward to juicy steaks.

Standing at the wrought iron railing, he lit a cigarette and tossed the pack onto the table. Studying the dazzling lights of the valley below, the flickering lights were like an early morning wake up call, reminding him that he had a busy day; a busy life ahead. When his cigarette was nothing but a glowing stub, he tossed it over the railing and down into the bushes of the canyon.

J.J. had polished off the screwdriver and had moved on. She came out to the terrace carrying two glasses of Dom Perignon with strawberries floating in them. She had changed out of her clothes into a robe and had pushed aside the opening of her robe, exposing her breasts. This wasn't going to be strictly an employer-employee relationship.

"You smoke?" J.J. asked, noticing the pack on the table as she walked toward him.

"That bother you?"

"You might rethink it," J.J. said, handing him a glass. She sat on a chaise lounge. "Join me?" How many visits to Dr. Wells' office would take to explain bringing this treat home?

He could see her nipples were as erect as he was. Squeezing in next to her, the towel around his waist slipped off.

She saw it as a warm invitation to ecstasy.

"You don't have much in the way of clothes, do you?"

"Like to travel light," Lucky said.

"Tomorrow you take my credit card and go shopping."

"No argument from me," he said. So, was this what his future held?

She slowly ran her tongue across his lips, drinking in droplets of champagne that lagged behind. "Let's go inside," she said.

"Move out of the way, cat," he said, as they walked into the bedroom. The cat snarled at him and jumped down.

"Her name is Bonbon. Careful with her, she's shy to new people."

J.J. reached her arm over, opening the top drawer of the nightstand. "Pick whichever one you want," she said, matter-of-factly, nodding at him to look in the drawer.

A cornucopia of condoms. Ribbed. Non-ribbed. Packaged in colorful foil. He caught a glimpse of some the well-marketed names. Midnight Ecstasy. Sun Has Risen. Grass Romp. Orange Juice. Caught off guard by her well-supplied pharmacy of products, he wasn't surprised, though he usually just carried one in his wallet.

"You're at my house now, honey. No condom. No sex. Make the right choice 'cause I'm ready," she said, taking another sip of the expensive bubbly.

"I didn't say I wasn't going to use one."

"That's good." She set the glass down, and toyed with

her nipple as he put the condom on. She glanced down at her body. She couldn't help but admire how firm, smooth and flawless she was. She looked amazing, and she knew it.

He watched her play with her nipples. Her eyes were dark, determined and experienced, nothing like—Oh, how he loved those innocent eyes. But he didn't want to think about that now. This woman was spread out in front of him like a Penthouse centerfold.

"You ready for me?" he asked, but he already knew the answer to that one.

"Screw me, baby." This man was a gift from above. How did she get so lucky? No wonder he was called that.

He entered her gently.

She wrapped her flawless legs–courtesy of Mrs. Lee's Hair and Nail Salon–around his tanned, muscular back. She stroked his back, while her tongue met his.

He thrust his hips repeatedly until she trembled, shut-tered, and screamed obscenities that he had never heard a woman say before.

She was more than satisfied, and fell asleep on top of him, pinning him down.

His desire had also been fulfilled, but it was just sex for him. No feeling. No emotion. It was business sex.

Afterwards, he got out of bed and retreated to the kitchen, stepping on Bonbon's tail, causing her to screech. He leaned down to grab the cat, but she retaliated with a slap from piercing claws, leaving a bloody scratch on his hand. "Bitch," he said as the feline ran out its cat door.

*   *   *

"You did what?" Gloria said, the next day. "I'm about to lose you, I'm in an elevator." The cell phone reception was full of static. Maybe she didn't hear her correct.

Gloria was straddling her briefcase, a cup of Starbucks coffee in her hand, and hoping there wouldn't be an earthquake before she got out. That was one drawback to having an office in a high-rise of the San Francisco financial district.

Gloria's law office of Bender, Baines and Harwood was one of many businesses in the towering building. Her office was on the twentieth floor. Every day she dreaded the trip up and down the claustrophobic lift.

The thirty-floor building was built on solid rock, or so Gloria liked to believe, since rock sounded safe. Also, it was better than where J.J. worked, down the peninsula in a fourteen-floor office building built on landfill. During an earthquake the phenomenon of liquefaction could occur, reminding architects not to build where there should be water. That could topple even the sturdiest of buildings.

J.J. was always bragging to Gloria about the great view from her smaller complex. Sure, J.J.'s office had an unobtrusive view of the bay, but when going down in a quake, who cares?

Sitting in her Nomadic office, her legs, browned courtesy of the tanning booth, were propped up on her desk. J.J. felt satisfied, better than a long soak in the mud baths at Calistoga.

"And his name isn't Lucky, it's Lane. Lane Lawson."

"He sounds pretty lucky, if you ask me. What do you know about him?"

"For starters, I know he's the best fuck I've ever had."

"Oh, that's a great reason to invite a total stranger into your house, into your life, worse yet into your business."

Gloria finally reached her own office, filled with waiting clients concerned with corporate legal issues for her to unravel. They always thought their problems were the ones that needed immediate and utmost attention over anyone else's. That was obvious. She needed a vacation.

"You're just jealous, that's all." J.J. said. "I'll talk to you later." She hung up the phone and buzzed for Lane.

"Get me John Dunn on the phone? You'll find his number in your computer."

"Sure thing, babe," Lucky said.

"By the way, Lane, let's get one thing straight, at the office, I'm Miss Jones."

That bitch. But, with the title of Administrative Assistant, he made himself at home at a desk in a cubicle just outside her office. He didn't have the view of the gleaming bay as she did. But, that was just a timing factor; of this he was certain.

Lucky was going to become one of the movers and shakers that sat in Chez Von over a three-hour lunch, plotting his next IPO. Even if in the interim it meant being J.J.'s prostitute.

Chapter Six

The persistent ringing of the phone echoed throughout the airy, Victorian house in the Marina district of San Francisco. Motionless, Gabriel's drained body was curled up into a comforting fetal position on the bed. He held a pillow over his head, trying unsuccessfully to block the irritation.

Law student Gabriel Fuentes felt like grabbing it and throwing it across the room until it silenced. His body told him it was still the middle of the night, even though the brightness of the morning fog filtering through the bay window discredited his belief.

After working a long shift at the law office of Bender, Baines and Harwood, where he interned, he spent what was left of the night reading and cramming for an exam in his Contracts class. He had the house to himself until Robbie came home from a play or musical, or something. Gabriel didn't know or care, since he hadn't kept up with the acting crowd.

The constant ringing convinced him a determined caller was at the other end. Whoever it was, kept calling back, even after the voice mail automatically picked up.

Knocking over a glass of flat ginger ale, he cleared the morning frog out of his throat. Why had he chosen law school in the first place?

"Hello," he whispered in a wispy voice, trying not to sound sleepy. How he hoped it wasn't someone at the office, especially Gloria Harwood, Senior Law Partner. No, couldn't be her. She would never waste her time calling him, a peon clerk.

"Robbie there?"

The female voice was barely audible, but Gabriel knew it wasn't the office, and he was glad the intruder hadn't wanted to talk to him. His internship at Bender, Baines and Harwood kept him insanely busy, and he was hoping for a short break, maybe even going back to sleep for a treasured additional fifteen minutes.

"Is he there?" The voice was louder.

Now, he recognized the voice as Heather Kane's. Gabriel knew that Robbie helped Heather study for her college classes, and in return, she drove him to his acting auditions. After his license was suspended for a drunk driving incident. They had a strange relationship. One that was difficult to understand. But, he already had enough on his plate without getting in the middle of the two pied pipers. They were stuck together like super glue, it seemed.

"Just a second," he said, needing to put on his eyeglasses so he could think better. Reaching for the case, he pulled out his tortoise-shelled glasses and placed them on his surgically enhanced nose. Gabriel looked over at the clock radio. Six thirteen. No wonder he was so tired. He'd planned on sleeping in, missing his morning classes, take his exam in the afternoon and be at the office by two. Now his precisely planned day was thrown off-kilter.

Heather was thirty miles over the hill in Sea Breeze. A cold, untouched cup of tea in a ceramic mug with a blue dolphin as a handle was near her hand. She hadn't slept all night, having watched every second of the clock change.

Winslow was in the corner of the room, curled up on a sheepskin rug Lucky had bought for him. He hadn't been the same since Lucky left. Roaming around the duplex, his broad nose sniffing for his old pal's scent, but Lucky was gone. The dog lay on the rug for hours, waiting for his return.

"Robbie?" Gabriel yelled out. "He's not here, Heather. Sorry."

"Can you tell him I called?"

"Sure. Anything I can do?" He regretted the words as soon as they spilled out. He hadn't wanted to get involved. Didn't matter much that Robbie was fond of Heather, Gabriel thought she was a flake and couldn't figure out what

Robbie saw in her.

"No, never mind. I just wanted to talk to him about something."

"I'll give him the message."

Holding a floral bouquet in one hand and a newspaper under his armpit, Robbie punched in the security code and entered the house. He loved his morning walk. Today was going to be one of those gorgeous California days that made you glad to be alive.

"Hold on, Heather, I think I hear him." Gabriel tossed aside the striped bed sheets, exposing his firm chest decorated with a few wiry hairs. He knew he would have to actually get out of bed so Rob and Heather could make their soul connection. Sleeping had become a distant fantasy.

Gabriel glanced at himself in the mirror as he left the bedroom and noticed how his two-day stubble and unruly hair was the epitome of how he felt. He thought his face looked older than his twenty-five years. Fine lines around his espresso-colored eyes added to his aged feeling, but Robbie always assured him that he was as hot as ever.

"Shit," Gabriel said, accidentally stubbing his toe against the wooden leg of the antique sofa. "Shit, shit, shit."

"You okay there, Gabe?" Robbie asked, laughing. "You look like the Easter bunny on a pogo stick." He tossed the flowers and paper down onto the antique entry table.

"I'm perfect. Your girlfriend is on the phone."

"Very funny. You mean Heather?"

"Who else? She sounds upset." Gabriel made the assessment, even though he barely remembered answering the phone. He was, after all, an attorney in training, and it was his job to size up people and their situations, even when half-asleep.

Gabriel grabbed the newspaper as he headed to the bathroom. After cleaning up, he hoped he could at least pretend to be awake.

Fearing the worst, Robbie went into their bedroom to

take the call. He wanted privacy. Had someone died? Been in a car accident?

"Heather, what is it?" Robbie nervously asked as he leaned over, noticing the spilled liquid on the nightstand. He wiped it up with the baggy sleeve of his gray hooded sweatshirt. Sitting on the king-sized bed, he unzipped the sweatshirt, and claimed an oversized pillow, holding it against his chest.

"He walked out on me."

"Oh, Heather—" Following a long pause, Robbie finally spoke. "That bastard, I don't know what you ..." But, before he could finish, he stopped himself. What was done couldn't be reversed. Negativity wouldn't solve anything. "Have you told your parents?"

"Tell my parents? You've got to be kidding," Heather said in disbelief, swirling her index finger around the cold tea. Looking out the window, she noticed that hummingbirds were at a feeder that was almost empty.

"I just thought ..." Robbie started to say. He knew it had been an empty question, but thought it should be asked nonetheless.

"I told you about my parents." Heather said, taking a piece of toilet paper out of the pocket of her terrycloth robe. She wiped her nose. How could her life go from perfection to disaster in such a short time?

"Yeah, you're right, Heather." Robbie watched Gabriel emerge from the bathroom. His wild, brown hair now combed and tamed. The newspaper was neatly folded under his arm with the sports section on top. His growled expression replaced with a smile.

"I'll be ready when you get here," Robbie said. Then hung up. He'd have to reschedule his day to accommodate her, but that's what friends did for each other.

Robbie sat on the edge of the bed and through the open door watched his lover, who was standing bare-chested wearing pajama bottoms in front of the TV in the formal living room. The remote control in his hand, he channel-surfed. From MSNBC to CNN to the local Channel 2, Robbie's personal favorite. As he watched Gabriel, he thought about how his life was comparatively uncomplicated, and how grateful he was because of it.

Robbie thought about what he needed to do next, and it wasn't going to be easy.

Chapter Seven

"Be at my office. Eleven-thirty sharp." John Dunn, venture capitalist extraordinaire, was pleased. He was sure his latest investment was going to make him a lot of money. When someone like Billy Sanger also chose to invest in it, the deal can't go wrong.

"I'll be there at eleven-twenty-nine." J.J. was flying so high, she wouldn't even need a car to get there.

"Lucky?" J.J. called out from her office.

"I'm on a call," he said back, annoyed as he glanced outside his office. People were constantly patrolling the hallway it seemed. Snoops.

"That's right," Lucky said into the phone. "Marble headstone with angel wings above her name." It was expensive, but it was the least he could do to fulfill the promise he had made for his mother's grave.

J.J. stood in the doorway and observed Lucky. His body moved with ease, as if he were unaware of how gorgeous he was. He was wearing a white long-sleeve Polo shirt she gave him. His pants were the same ones he used to wear waiting tables. She'd have to do something about that. But his face was flawless, other than a small scar under one eye. No big deal. That could be taken care of with one quick trip to the plastic surgeon. Otherwise, his face looked as if he were an after picture for a makeover. He hadn't shaved this morning, so a bit of stubble showed

"That's right, Marie Lukovich," Lucky said. Then he hung up.

"Lucky?" J.J. asked in a teasing manner. "Hope that's not a personal call?"

"Does it matter? Besides, in the office, it's Lane." He laughed.

"But, darling, you are my lucky star, my good luck

charm," she said walking up to him. She was drawn to him. Stroking his back in a motion she'd learned from her private masseuse, a man named Sven, even though he hailed from Phoenix.

Lucky ignored his impulse to turn around and run out of the office, back to Heather and Sea Breeze. Instead, he took a new pack of cigarettes out of his desk drawer. His stomach growled.

"You were restless last night," J.J. said. He'd tossed around in bed all night, sweating and pretending to sleep. J.J. figured it would take him a while to adjust to the new surroundings.

"I was just hot," he said. He hadn't slept at all. He struggled with sleep until the morning sun shined into his eyes, forcing him out of bed. The guilt over leaving Heather and before her, his damned old man. The haunting memories would never go away. A vision of him dead kept poisoning Lucky's mind.

"You must be hot-blooded," J.J. said.

More like cold-blooded, he thought.

"Listen, doll," she said, sitting on his desk. "I have a very important appointment, and while I'm gone, you need to go to Janie in Human Resources. She has some forms for you to fill out."

"Forms?" Lucky dug his thumb into the cellophane wrapper of the new cigarette package.

"Just new employee stuff. All very basic. Your stock options, all that. You couldn't have joined our company at a better time. We're going out soon, you know."

"Going out?"

"Darling," she purred, "don't toy with me, when our offering goes public, you'll be a very rich man. I can see to it, but only if you play your cards right."

"I play a good hand of poker."

"I knew you were in the game," she said. "By the way, H.R. will also go over the benefit package, and there's something else, oh yeah, medical insurance."

"Oh?" Tossing the plastic wrap into a garbage can under his desk, he missed, landing it on the floor instead. Healthy guys didn't need medical insurance.

"Benefits here are excellent." She thought he was the best benefit of all.

"By the way, Lane, this is a smoke-free environment, like all public buildings in California, but then you should know that having worked in a restaurant. Go outside to smoke. When I come back, I'm expecting an important call from my P.R. people. Put it through as soon as it comes in. Oh, I almost forgot. Before I go, there's one other thing."

Her full breasts were barely covered by her clinging blouse, the buttons ready to pop to expose her chest. Her skirt rode up her curvaceous hips as she leaned close to him.

Papers that he had on his desk in an attempt to look busy got pushed to the floor. She put her arms around his neck, pulling him into her waiting lips.

"In the office?" he asked, in between kisses.

"Why not?"

"Don't you have an appointment?"

"You're right. See, that's why I hired you, to keep me on top of things."

That woman, Lucky thought. No wonder she couldn't keep an assistant.

Picking up her briefcase by the strap, she headed toward the door, then turned around, her dark, shiny hair flowing as if she were doing a shampoo commercial. Reaching into her pocket, she pulled out a set of keys, and tossed them to him. "Here."

He looked surprised as he caught him. "What are these for?"

Her tongue circled her lips in an alluring tease. "Lucky, my welcome-on-board gift is waiting for you outside. P.S. I'll give you a hint. It's black."

Shit. This woman was on fire. Had he gotten more than

he bargained for? Before he could think about it, the phone on his desk rang.

"Answer it," J.J. said, waving her manicured fingers, then disappearing down the hallway.

"Hello?" Lucky's words were curt.

"This is Janie in H.R. Are you coming down to my office or what? I've been waiting for you."

"Crap."

"What?" Janie hated working in H.R. All the redundant paperwork made her testy. They were supposed to be on a hiring freeze this close to the offering, but Jennifer Jones did what she wanted.

"I'll be there as soon as I can." But, as soon as he could, was not anytime soon. At least not until he saw what the keys were for.

He repeatedly pressed the button for the elevator. "Open. Open. Open, you damned door!" The sweat in his palms was enough to bathe the keys.

When the elevator doors finally opened, two women were chatting inside. He figured the one with the big tits and wearing a short miniskirt, high-heels, and a smile, to be just his type, even though she was a brunette. The other, the redhead, had possibilities as well. His fickle feelings between J.J., Heather and every other red-blooded woman was frustrating and confusing. Yet, he was young. Why not play the field? Especially since most of the playing was in his mind.

"Did you see that writing on that car's windshield?" the redhead asked the brunette, but turning toward Lucky.

"You talking to me?" Lucky asked, shrugging his shoulders. He had no idea what they were talking about.

"You're new here, aren't you?" the redhead asked. "You work for Jennifer Jones, right?"

"That's right."

"The woman's a powerhouse," she said. "You landed a good job. Not to mention, your timing. Pretty impeccable, if you ask me."

Yeah, well, I hadn't asked you, Lucky thought.

"Right when we're going public? How'd you get the job, anyway?"

"I—" Lucky never thought he'd have to explain to people. Was that necessary? Did people need or want to know? Maybe they only hired college graduates. Maybe Heather was right. Why else would they be suspicious? Curious if that's what Janie wanted, he wondered if she wanted to see his nonexistent green card too. Why would they even need all that information?

The brunette saved Lucky from having to answer, "I wouldn't want that job. Workin' for the dragon lady. No thanks. I don't care if she is president. What's your name, cutie pie?"

"Luc—I mean, Lane. Lane Lawson." These questions would need rehearsing so that his dumbfounded looks would-n't shine around every time someone inquired.

"I'm Abby, short for Abigail."

"And this is Candace."

Lucky thought the people who worked at Nomadic, other than a few nerds in accounting, looked as if they were clones. Young, beautiful, perfect bodies, and other than J.J., he hadn't seen any other forty-year-olds at the company, even the Vice Presidents were young. He'd even heard a rumor that once someone hit forty, they were permanently laid off. Nice word for fired, so it seemed.

The elevator stopped at the next floor, but there was no one waiting as the doors opened. They stood in awkward silence, waiting for the doors to close.

"Well, it's nice to meet you, ladies," Lucky said, jiggling the keys in his hand. He was trying to stay calm, but the ele-vator was so slow.

"Lane, you have something on your face," Abby said, leaning toward him, tickling his face with her fingertips.

A chill ran down his back. She looked as if she belonged in Playboy. Lucky softly put his hand around her fingers. His stomach growled, and he let go of her hand.

"Hungry?" Abby asked, running her fingers in a circle around her firm stomach, causing the top of her blouse to lift off showing her pierced belly button ring.

"It looks like somebody's been nibbling on you."

Lucky glanced at his reflection in the mirrored elevator walls. He wasn't sure what was redder, the red lipstick smudge or his embarrassed face. "Shit."

The giggling women got off on the Second Floor with hot gossip they couldn't wait to spread like a computer virus.

*   *   *

"Hey, new guy, where's the fire?" The fifty-year-old anomaly Wayne Darby from accounting said as Lucky hurriedly left the elevator when it reached Ground Level.

"Nowhere, just taking a smoke break." Realizing he left the smokes upstairs, he wondered if quitting was a good idea.

"That's a bad habit, you know."

"Whatever." Like he cared if this guy thought he shouldn't smoke. All he cared about was the presumed black beauty that would smoke down the freeway.

The glistening Porsche was parked near the building entrance in a handicap spot.

Lucky briefly read over the dealer's sticker price list which was glued to the driver's side window, loaded with every conceivable option. As he walked around the car in disbelief, he was aware of the group of women that had gathered two flights up, peering out the window.

Abby, Candace and four other women all worked in different departments at Nomadic had different personalities, likes and dislikes. But, they had one thing in common, gossiping. At that moment, they watched the lunchtime entertainment below as Lane checked out his new toy.

"So, Abby, do you think he's the Lucky Star?" Candace asked.

"I'll say he is." The yearning hadn't left her since she felt the electricity created when he touched her; enough to keep California lit for the winter. "He can be my assistant anytime."

"You gotta be president first."

"Minor detail."

The women laughed, then went their separate ways.

*   *   *

Lucky opened the car with the remote control, hopped in and slid onto the driver's seat as if it had been custom created just for him. The engine started smoothly. After glancing in the rear view mirror, he put his left foot on the clutch and reversed the car out of the parking spot. A careful and safe driver, he was. Laughing, he thought about how J.J. must assume he had a driver's license. What a fool she was.

Stepping hard on the gas pedal, he roared out of the Nomadic Software parking lot. He turned on the windshield wipers and kept squirting the water until the red lipstick scrawl, Lucky Star, was removed from the windshield.

Lucky merged onto Highway 101 at a smooth ninety miles an hour. This car gave him the status he needed, for now, anyway.

He'd drive up to the city, do a few laps, then drive down the coast to show Heather his new baby.

Chapter Eight

"Your eleven-thirty is here," Taylor Burke said in an instant message to her boss, John Dunn.

For the twenty-nine-year-old, today was just another day working for the top venture capitalist in the industry. Except that he was anything but typical, and her days were anything but ordinary. Turning to the woman who was pacing in the waiting room, she doubted the visitor was happy. "Would you like a cup of coffee?"

"No thanks. Is he ready for me?" she asked, cutting Taylor off in mid-sentence.

Bitch. "You'll have to wait. He's on a conference call with India." She didn't know why she told her that. Phone calls and meetings were always confidential, but this lady rattled her nerves.

Fuck India, J.J. thought. She needed to make her own conference call to India. Suspicious that her people there were slacking off, and slacking off was not allowed when Nomadic Software was on track to go public. She knew that she needed to make the overseas trip, but hated the long flight and hated getting sick once she got there. The whole idea made her feel unpleasant, itchy, dirty, needing a shower. It reminded her that she needed more toilet paper at home. Taking her handheld computer out of the side pocket of her briefcase, she updated her e-shopping list, which was connected directly to her grocery shopping service.

Her cell phone rang, but she turned it off, wanting to clear her head to clarify everything she needed to cover with John Dunn. As she waited, she sorted through a stack of current business journals.

Finally, the small signal light icon on the screen changed from red to green on Taylor's desk, going unnoticed. She'd been busy getting ready to leave for lunch, rummaging through her purse looking for lipstick in anticipation of her lunch date with a Forty-Niner football linebacker.

Just one of the perks of working for her boss. Through the prestige of being John Dunn's right-hand woman, she was able to meet fascinating people daily. The men, single or married, asked her out for lunch, dinner, cruise on the bay, drive to Monterey, whatever she wanted to do on any given day.

Today, she was meeting the football player for lunch at Josephine's, near an upscale shopping center, just down the road from the office. She never had to pay for lunch with the list of prospective dates. The backlog could carry her well into the spring, and perhaps to her own summer wedding. If she found the right mate.

"Is he ready for me, yet?" J.J. asked, putting down the latest copy of Technology Week. She had already read the article about John Dunn, his errant personality and quirks set him apart from the rest of the moneyed suits.

John Dunn didn't fit the mold of a Sand Hill V. C. That's what drew J.J. to him in the first place. She didn't want typical, she wanted results that would set her and Nomadic apart from the heard of high-tech companies that clamored for funding. All with the ultimate goal of going public and making big game winnings.

John Dunn's office of Dunn Capital was located on famed Sand Hill where most of the Godlike venture capitalists reigned over the valley. They were the ones who steered the herds, the ones with the true power. With their hotly sought funding, they determined who would be in business for another year and who would have to start selling off assets.

She didn't know why she was so jittery. This, of course, wasn't the first time she'd met him, but her stomach was turning and her nerves were out of control. She reached into her purse and found the last of her pills, swallowing them without benefit of a drink.

J.J. hadn't seen his office yet; he'd been having the place

remodeled. Until now, it had been a dusty construction zone. They'd previously met either at Gloria's office, Nomadic or Chez Von, and she was anxious to see what the office looked like for the man that had given Nomadic six million dollars.

She'd heard about his houses. Besides his sprawling ranch, he had a multimillion-dollar estate overlooking Pebble Beach Golf Course. But he didn't play golf like the other V. C.s, wooing investment bankers. The truth being, he never even went to his Pebble Beach mansion, preferring to stay locally at his ranch in Los Altos Hills. The only irons he played with were shoehorns.

The highest scale of meeting him was to be invited to his ranch. J.J. hadn't had that honor yet. But she was getting closer. This time his office, next time she'd be at the ranch roping calves, or whatever he did there.

As she sat and waited her turn, she wondered if the office would live up to her expectation. She'd heard about the construction of it through the valley grapevine. Word was that he had an unobstructed view of a local university tower, and a panoramic view of the San Francisco Bay beyond that.

Having located her compact and tube of lipstick, Taylor applied the mocha color that the clerk at Nordstrom's assured her suited her dark complexion, but now she disagreed and planned on returning it, even though it'd been used. Fixing her bangs, which she also disliked, she told herself she had to find a new hairdresser, someone that knew how to work with her coarse hair.

"Well?" J.J. asked, glaring at the woman who seemed more preoccupied with herself than those of the client. At this moment, going into John's office would be ideal.

"Oh, sorry," she said, putting her compact down, noticing the green flashing signal on her computer monitor. "You can go in now, Miss Jones."

"Thank you." Bitch. J.J. entered the Holy Grail of Sand Hill, John Dunn's office.

"Welcome," John Dunn said, reaching out his well-toned arm with his shirtsleeves rolled up to take J.J.'s hand. In his forties, standing at least six-foot-three, he had the physique of a twenty-year-old. His autumn-brown hair, the color of oak leaves, had specks of gray at the temples; he wore it just below his ears. On his feet, cowboy boots.

"Oh, I'm sorry," J.J. said, horrified when she realized as she shook his hand that her palm was sweaty. She wished there was an antiperspirant for hands. Noticing scratches on his tanned arm, she scoured her brain for small talk. "Got a cat too, huh?" Why was she so freaking nervous? Good Lord, why would she assume the scratches came from a cat?

"No, rose bushes." He wasn't one for small talk. They had last minute details to go over before the offering.

"Lovely," she said. Bending her head down, her stomach was doing somersaults.

"It's a beauty, isn't it?" He'd assumed her lowered head meant she was admiring the Native American rug. "It's one-of-a-kind."

She feared the one-of-a-kind rug was about to get some new colors on it. She felt dizzy. Maybe it wasn't her stomach. Maybe they were having an earthquake?

"Now, Miss Jones, shall we get on with our meeting?"

Before she could answer, she threw up on the irreplaceable rug.

Chapter Nine

"Thanks for coming with me," Heather said as she pulled into the parking lot of the Medical Center.

Robbie glanced at his friend and felt frustrated. "No problem, but, is there anything else I can say to change your mind?" After having spent the better part the morning carrying on a one-way conversation with a stubborn Heather, he was at his wits' end.

"No, I told you, I don't want to talk about it," Heather said as she parked in the last open slot. She hoped Robbie had enough cash to pay for the parking on the way out, 'cause she didn't have a dollar on her.

Once inside the doctor's office, Heather's body filled with tension.

"Fill out these forms," the receptionist said, handing Heather a clipboard laden with papers.

Heather filled out the paperwork in rapid time, handed them back and then waited. After forty-five minutes, the door opened.

"You can come in now, Mrs. Kane."

"It's Miss."

"Right. You can go into that examining room. Get into the gown. I'll come back and take your vitals, then Dr. Odenmeir will see you."

Heather complied, again.

The nurse returned, took her vitals, and Heather waited for the doctor. Seemed like an eternity. She wondered what Robbie was up to in the waiting room.

"So, how long have you worked for Dr. Orifice?" a bored Robbie with elbows on the counter, asked the receptionist.

"It's Dr. Odenmeir." She was not amused. Forget that this guy thought he was being funny. She shut the glass partition while he was saying something, she didn't know what.

That was rude, Robbie thought as he sat down in the waiting room, glad that he'd printed out his e-mail before leaving the house. He'd been in a rush and hadn't had time to read his daily barrage of messages. Glancing through the stack, he read the one from his casting agent, concerning an audition for a new play in New York.

His stomach growled. After the doctor's appointment, he wanted to take Heather out for crepes. Off Mission Street, a real hole in the wall, the best kind of eatery. This one was run by a couple of ex-dot-com-ers. Refuges from the Silicon Valley Internet boom that went bust. Since closing down their web company, which Gabriel's law firm handled the paperwork for, the men went into another kind of food business. Their business plan was simple, with an immediate cash flow. Profit depended on how many crepes they sold each day, not how many cans of pet food they'd wrongly anticipated the world would buy.

Robbie's mouth watered as he thought about which crepe he would order, orange-mango or shrimp. Then he remembered he'd forgotten to call the restaurant to tell Jean-Marc he wouldn't be in.

"Do you have a phone I can use?" he asked, knocking on the frosted glass partition. "I don't have my cell phone with me."

"Sure," the receptionist said, sliding open the enclosure. "Long as it's local." Her accusatory eyes glared at him as if he'd committed a crime.

Local as the crow flies. For some reason, Chez Von had a different area code. Robbie never understood how so many cities so close to each other could be so far apart in phone communications.

*   *   *

The doctor was gentle in his examination of Heather.

The nurse stood nearby, and Heather felt self-conscious.

"Everything seems fine. Would you like to see if we can hear the heartbeat?" Dr. Odenmeir asked.

Though Heather would have loved to, she was afraid. Hearing the heartbeat would create too special a bond between mother and child. That she couldn't risk, no matter how wonderful the experience might be. "No, doctor. I just can't. Not now."

"Well, in that case, you can get up now," Dr. Odenmeir said, thinking she'd seemed a little emotional, but that was normal for someone in her condition. "My nurse here will give you a book to read." He sat down on a short stool with wheels, adjusting his bifocals, then wrote in her chart.

"I can't have this baby," Heather said softly.

"Of course, you can. Millions of women do it every day." His eyes never looked away from what he was writing.

"I'm not married."

He chuckled. "Since when has that been a requirement?"

Standing up, he put the chart down on the nearby counter top that was filled with jars of cotton balls and Q-tips. "We're done here, Miss Kane, you can get dressed now."

"You don't understand—"

Reaching into the pocket of his lab coat, he pulled out a prescription pad. "I'm giving you some prenatal vitamins." Glancing at the clock, he thought about making a mad dash out of the office for lunch before his afternoon round of patients. There was never enough time on his busy days, but every day was a busy one. He had considered retiring at the end of the year, but when his wife died unexpectedly of an aneurysm, traveling the world suddenly seemed pointless.

Heather felt as if she was in kindergarten again and the teacher wouldn't let her speak during circle time. "Dr. Odenmeir, you're not listening to me. I'm not having this baby." She'd thought she and Lucky had been careful. She wanted children someday, just not now.

"That's utter nonsense, my dear."

"You don't know the whole story." The stiff paper beneath her crinkled and was amplified by the slightest shift of her body.

"Would you like me to talk to the father?" Scratching the bald spot on the back of his head, he was at least half-concerned. The hair transplants hadn't taken, and his scalp was as itchy as a bad sunburn.

For the first time in days, a smile came to Heather's face. Dr. Odenmeir must have thought Robbie was the father? "The man who came in with me isn't the father."

"What did you want to do then?"

"I want it to be over," she said, her bare feet dangling off the end of the examining table. She started to shiver. The gown she'd been wearing was soft against her skin, but flimsy from too many washing, and she'd wished she'd brought her sweater. Now, she had to go to the bathroom.

"Is that what you want? To terminate the pregnancy?"

"Yes."

"Go ahead and get dressed."

"I thought it could be done today," Heather said, sliding off the examining table.

"Oh, no, dear. I don't do that procedure. I'll refer you out. Get dressed. Meet me in my office, and we'll discuss it. Bring in your friend if you'd like."

"Thank you, doctor," Heather said, the tan having dissipated from her face.

Dr. Odenmeir went into his office, and took a drink from a cup of stale decaf. The mug, a gift from his late wife read, World's Best Husband. Sometimes the hardest part of being a doctor for him was being impartial, he tended to transfer personal feelings onto his patients.

After stopping in the bathroom, Heather went back into the waiting room. "The doctor's done with the exam, and wants to talk to me."

Robbie noticed that her face looked freshly washed,

though pale as milk. She had applied a light coat of clear lip-gloss. Her white pants were decorated with tiny silver sequins she'd glued on around the hem. He thought she could wear anything and make it look stylish. The turquoise-colored hal-ter-top had matching sequins around the neckline, and she was carrying her strappy sandals in her hand. Always the bare-foot girl.

"Okay," he said. "I'll wait."

"No, come with me," she said, almost pleading. "I wish this was over." Pulling her headband off, her hair danced onto her rounded shoulders. Her eyes were puffy and he wondered if she'd been crying.

"Doll, you're gonna be fine," Robbie said, feeling guilty for wanting to turn and run out. The odor of antiseptic was making his stomach churn.

Robbie thought she had a glow, an aura, to her and wondered if she should be an actor instead of him. Heather had always told him that he was talented, but he could see her drama over her silent feelings; feelings of pain, sorry and rejection by Lucky dumping her without a second thought, or so it seemed.

"Let's see what the guy has to say, Heather." He forced a smile as they walked into Dr. Odenmeir's certificate-lined office.

"Have a seat, you two," the doctor said, gazing at Robbie.

"If your decision's been made, I'll give you a referral." Dr. Odenmeir handed Heather a piece of paper. He made a mental note to call his ailing mother, who had adopted him as an infant.

"Heather, think about this," Robbie whispered, his words, adamant. Maybe he and Gabriel could adopt the baby. Married parents. Divorced parents. Same sex parents. This was done all the time. Family was how they would be defined.

"Come on, think about this. Don't make a hasty deci-sion about her," Robbie urged.

"Her?"

"Or him?"

"Are you out of your mind?"

"I am of sound mind and body." Robbie noticed the doctor seemed to be ignoring them as he flipped through an address book.

"Robbie, you're crazy. What would Gabriel say?"

"He'd be all for it."

"Thank you, doctor," Heather said, ignoring Robbie. Making a decision to raise a child wasn't something decided on a whim. What was the matter with him? Taking the referral, she folded it and put it in her purse. Her decision had been made. And, it hadn't been made on a whim.

Standing up, she shook the doctor's hand, and glanced over at Robbie, his face read of disappointment. She had her own growing up to do. She'd been pretending to be an adult, yet she never felt so infantile.

Robbie hadn't spoken on their way out to the car. Preferring to drive barefoot, Heather tossed her sandals onto the floor of the back seat, noticing she needed to vacuum the dog hair. She couldn't even take care of something so simple, how'd she ever be expected to care for a child. Although she had to admit, if Lucky was still in the picture, it'd be a different story. Driving out of the parking lot, she turned to Robbie. "Did you want me to put the convertible top down?"

Robbie just glared to her, then finally spoke. "No, it's too hot. Besides, I forgot to put sunscreen on."

"You don't have to be so sarcastic."

"Who's being sarcastic?"

"I'll take you home."

"Heather, I wanted to at least take you to lunch. If you won't let me be the father of your baby, let me at least treat you."

"What a trade off."

"Head toward Mission Street."

"Eating is the last thing I feel like doing," she said, as she merged onto a busy boulevard. This was lunch hour for most folks, the time when harried people descended out of their high-rise office buildings and narrowly avoided getting run over by cars. Road rage was everywhere. Seemed as if driving through an intersection without waiting for more than one signal change was the style of the decade.

"What about it?" Robbie was persistent.

"About lunch?"

"Forget about lunch if you want. Just think about me and Gabe adopting the baby."

"I'm sure Gabe would just love having a crying baby around."

"Now, who's being sarcastic?"

"I don't know." She didn't want to discuss it anymore.

Abruptly changing lanes, she cut off a minivan. "Can you turn the radio off? It's giving me a bloody headache." She rubbed her right eye.

"Getting a migraine?" Robbie could always tell by the fuzzy look in her eyes.

"Maybe." All she knew was that her vision was blotchy, she felt as if she were on a dance floor with flashing strobe lights after too much to drink. Only she was in a car, hadn't had anything to drink, feeling as if her head were in a vise with someone tightening it until her ears bled.

"Where are your sunglasses?" Robbie asked, glancing at her, squinting.

"I don't know. Somewhere." She slammed on the brakes, as a taxicab cut smack in front of her.

"Put these on, Heather." He handed her his sunglasses.

Taking them, she put them on.

"Have you told, you know, the biological father?" He hated getting the words out, but felt it should be addressed.

"Why bother?"

"I don't like him any more than the next asshole, but maybe he has a right to know."

"Robbie." Heather was beyond annoyed. "I'm all talked

out. I've made my decision, and I'm not going to talk about it any more." Why had she asked Robbie to go with her to the doctor's appointment? That was a mistake for sure.

"You should talk to someone about this. Have you told your parents?"

"These glasses are nice." Changing the subject was a must. If she wasn't going to tell the baby's biological father, why would she tell her parents?

"Forget the glasses. I know this priest—well, he used to be a priest, but anyway, he counsels people."

"Who?"

"The guy I'm telling you about."

"Do you think this heat wave is going to continue?"

"He sort of separated himself from the Catholic Church."

"How do you sort of separate yourself from the Catholic Church?"

"He just left his parish one day in the suburbs. Distributed Communion then walked right out in the middle of Mass. Now he's in the city with his own church, you should see it. He wanted to work with the people more directly, one on one, without the bureaucracy. His name is Father Ted, and—"

"I'm not going to see Father Ted or any other man of the cloth." Becoming more irritated, Heather interrupted, her voice rising an octave higher with each syllable. "That's the end of it."

Her face felt flushed and her stomach did flip-flops. Having been on a Bay tour in high winds and becoming seasick, she felt sort of the same now. Opening the window hadn't helped. She pulled alongside a UPS truck in the far right lane. It was double-parked. Drivers behind her started honking their horns.

She leaned her throbbing head out the open window. "I'm gonna be sick." She threw up.

"You, okay? Move over, girl, let me drive." He got out

of the car and ran around to the driver's side, being careful not to step in the vomit. At least it got outside instead of in the car, though the door was covered with it. His pricey sunglasses had fallen off her face and landed lens-side down in the liquid. No way was he touching those. Didn't care how much they cost.

Waiting for Heather to move over to the passenger side, he turned to the impatient driver in the car behind them. The one yelling obscenities.

"Hush up," Robbie said, waving his hand. "Pregnant lady on board." He got into the car, which reeked of a combination of barf and sweat.

"Robbie, where are we going?"

"You'll see. In the meantime, take a nap, darlin'. Robert is taking over." With a gentle hand, he patted her on her knee and noticed she wasn't wearing her seat belt. Probably too uncomfortable, what her being pregnant and all, but she needed to fasten it.

"Well, Robert, you're not supposed to be driving." Her voice softened as she leaned back into the seat, closing her eyes.

"Don't worry about it, Heather. I'm a good driver. Besides, you know I don't drink anymore. But, you better put on your seat belt, anyway."

After clasping the miserable belt, Heather realized how sleepy she felt, pregnancy made her tired. She hoped that when she woke up, her life would be different.

Without the benefit of sunglasses, Robbie squinted, almost blinded by the reflection of the sun hitting a car's rear window in front of them.

*   *   *

"You must keep your arms and legs in at all times, as long as you're in this place of mine's." Benjamin Washington, or Benny as he was usually known, sang in rhyme. The fifty-eight-year-old cable car grip man had wrinkles on his face as deep as the Grand Canyon, but a heart just as big.

The loud noise of the trolley as he prepared to descend the steep hill drowned out his hoarse voice. He was like a school yard supervisor to the throngs of out-of-towners who thought it was fun, while not realizing the danger of waving their extremities around carelessly when standing on the outside platform ledge of the cable car, hanging onto to a pole with their free arm.

People clamored to ride on the outside portion of the car, inadvertently or not, pushing each other out of the way when it stopped to pick up passengers who had been waiting in long lines for the cable car to arrive. Folks didn't come to San Francisco to sit on the inside of the car; they wanted to be out where their hair was brushed by the wind. Where they felt exhilarated to be alive.

Benny operated the braking system and rang the brass bells, and the conductor collected fares.

"Ring the bell again," a tourist turned and said, oblivious that the bell sound was actually a form of communication, each succession of bells having had a particular meaning.

Having won the annual Bell Ringing Contest five years running, Benny pretended he was the conductor of a symphony and that the city was his audience.

When Benny went to bed at night with his faithful wife of forty years in her flannel nightgown, he still heard the clanging in his sleep. He figured that's what working on the cable cars for eighteen years did to a man.

A polite man, Benny would smile when tourists took a picture of him. He figured his ugly mug was in photo albums all across the country, if not the world. He was famous in a way, almost a celebrity.

Passengers on the cable cars, from Midwesterners on a budget to the well-dressed Nob Hill residents, couldn't help but be excited with the picturesque, panoramic views of the tall buildings. The bay was in the distance. Traveling hills so steep, the passengers couldn't see what was coming next, causing even the most stoic adults to squeal like their children did.

Cable car conductor Benjamin Washington always knew what was coming next. The route was memorized in the synapse of his brain. They neared the next intersection, and with his glove-covered Herculean hands, he squeezed the jaws of the grip lever, braking the cable car.

Benny glanced around at the full-to-capacity cable car. A large group, traveling together, an equal number of adults and children, were preoccupied, deciding where to go next, Coit Tower or Lombard Street. He'd heard someone say that they were from Minnesota and were in town with a high school marching band. Though the instruments were back at the hotel, they were loud and boisterous, might as well have brought the brass, too.

From the corner of his eye, a white guy, probably one of the chaperones, wearing a Bud Light tank top and khaki Bermuda shorts with his arm outstretched into the street, snapping pictures, caught his eye. "Sir, please don't do that," Benny urged. Having never had an accident, Benny prided his ability and his perfect safety record.

*   *   *

Robbie was pleased with himself. He was speeding through the streets at record time. Considering traffic was heavy, it was moving at a good clip.

And, he would find a way to convince Heather his plan was a sound one.

For once, the city was cooperating. The green lights were in his favor. Whistling, he even thought about pulling over and putting the convertible top down, after all. He glanced over at Heather who was asleep. Just an innocent girl who got herself into trouble, but he'd set things right.

Approaching the next intersection, he saw the "No Left

Turn" sign but ignored it. A nuisance, he thought, an unnecessary law thought up by people who probably never even drove in the city without an inkling about traffic flow reality.

Making an illegal left, he didn't see any cops around, and the street looked clear to him. This was quicker than driving around the block, especially since his destination was so close.

Turning the corner, he didn't see the flashing warning lights overhead. An oncoming cable car was right there.

The screeching sound of the car's tires on the hot asphalt was overshadowed by the horrified screams of the tourists.

Chapter Ten

Weaving in and out of traffic, the Porsche continued its northerly route.

After a quick stop for more smokes, Lucky had decided he wasn't hitting the brakes until he reached the city. Then, he'd take the scenic road with its peaks and valleys that followed the coastline south to see Heather. He couldn't wait to show her the new car, and how successful he appeared.

First, he'd drive around the city. Drive the hairpin turns down the World's Crookedest Street. Do it without using brakes, and set a new world record for speed. Guinness would have to reprint their latest edition to include him and his magnificent driving.

Shifting the gears as the transmission hummed like mating doves, he thought about his trip to America on the boat, in particular, what the sailors had said. Work hard. You'll be rewarded. He hadn't worked all that hard. He didn't consider sex work, and he'd already been rewarded with a car to-die-for.

Driving up one of the steeper hills, he laughed as he thought about how smooth the upward direction his life had taken. He leaned over and turned the volume up of the radio and sang along. "Hot town, summer in the city."

Each time he got to a summit of a hill, he glanced around at the contradictory view. From the blue, smooth as unscratched glass, bay to the jagged starkness of Alcatraz. An island of reminders that it wasn't of this world, but of a dark, black hole in the universe where prisoners had gone in and never returned, or so that was what he read.

The prison reminded him of his father. "What would you think of your son, Pop? I'm not the loser you accused me of being. Am I?" He wondered what happened that night, after he'd run away. Where had the old crumb been buried?

How he was mortified to think his father might be buried next to Lucky's mother. But he was probably in a pauper's grave. Surely in hell.

His unprotected dark eyes, somewhat hindered by the sun, were focusing on the dashboard and all the bells and whistles it offered, not on what was ahead of him down the road.

He looked up suddenly and shoved his foot to the brake pedal. The car fishtailed as it surrendered. Skidding, unable to do any more, he put his hands over his face and wondered if it was too late to add medical insurance. When the car stopped moving, he was within inches of the back of a motionless garbage truck.

"Yes," he screamed, his hands congratulating the steering wheel. The car was exemplary, perfect acceleration, perfect braking.

Glancing in the rear view mirror, he noticed not a hair out of place. He liked the gel that he'd used that morning and planned to buy more. Reaching onto the seat next to him. he pulled out a congratulatory cigarette for the trip back to the office, figuring he'd better take care of the damn paperwork.

Unable to see what was causing the traffic standstill, he lit the smoke, holding it in his lips while starting to back up the car. He sensed a presence and stopped to look up. A man who looked like he'd taken the wrong turn at Marine boot camp was staring at him. Lucky wondered what the cop with ironed uniform shirt and hairy knuckles wanted.

"Yes?" Lucky hoped the cop wasn't going to ask him for a driver's license.

"Where do you think you're going?" the cop asked, his voice as angry as if he'd just found out his wife had been cheating. Business was hard enough to keep the street clear for the emergency vehicles and to direct traffic, but when people started making their own driving rules, it became impossible.

"I gotta get out of here," Lucky said.

"Yeah, you and every other citizen." The rubber on the soles of his boots felt as if they were melting.

"You know," the cop said, "there's a fatality up there."

"Oh, yeah?" Lucky asked. Not that he cared. He looked at his watch, a gift from J.J. Not a Rolex, but a high-priced gold knockoff. "Damn," Lucky said, as he realized he wouldn't have time to do all he planned.

The cop glanced around. Traffic was a mess. He should run this guy's license. Probably had a ton of unpaid tickets. An outstanding warrant, maybe. He wiped the beads of sweat off the bridge of his nose from under the rim of the wire-framed sunglasses that were pinching his sunburned nose. Today was one of those rare days in the city of sweltering heat. Times like this, he'd earned every hour of his pay.

The police officer's thoughts were on the mess of twisted metal ahead. Wondering if they'd gotten the people out, he didn't have time for this jerk. "There's another ambulance coming through, you'll have to wait. We'll be redirecting traffic once it's through."

"Thank you, officer," Lucky said, grateful the cop took a walk. Then inhaling his cigarette, he blew the smoke out, aiming for the memory of the cop's ruddy face.

Walking toward the accident site, the cop patted his nightstick, a habitual gesture he was almost unaware of. Glancing back at the guy in the Porsche, he detested showoffs like that. Probably some high-tech gazillionaire asshole. He would've liked to have issued him a ticket for just being alive. But, he had priorities. Keeping the street clear for one. The smart ass would be punished enough having to sit there in the heat and wait in the traffic jam while the Volkswagen was untangled from a cable car.

After the cop disappeared, Lucky backed the car, then felt it bumped a car behind him.

"Son-of-a-bitch," the driver said, jumping out of his Geo Metro. His right fist throbbed as he clenched it harder and harder while approaching the Porsche. He was ready to grab the guy's throat and strangle him. No one touched his mama's car, not in this lifetime, then lived to tell about it.

"Christ," Lucky said, glancing at the guy, who was in all likelihood an escapee from San Quentin. Wearing a baggy, muscle shirt, Lucky could see, not just a little heart tattoo like he had, but a large black cross with a dagger stabbed through it on the escapee's arm. No, he wasn't an escapee, Lucky smirked, he must be a wrestling championship holder.

"What's your problem?" Lucky asked. Man, this brute was someone to be taken seriously. Lucky would be terrified of bumping into him in a dark alley. "I barely touched you," Lucky said, forcing a smile.

The guy reached his hands into the car, just as Lucky threw his smoldering cigarette out, brushing by the man's ear. "Shit," the guy said as he felt his ear singe. "I'll kick your ass."

"Not today, pal." Maneuvering the car back and forth, Lucky felt more threatened than he wanted to let on. If this hothead smelled his fear, who knew what would happen? Freeing himself from the champ and traffic jail, he made a U-turn, driving up on the sidewalk, speeding down the street to make his own escape.

His cell phone rang. Another gift from J.J.

"Where are you? Get back to the office."

"I got tied up in traffic. I'll be there as soon as I can."

"Make it quick."

Shit. Now, the opportunity to see Heather was gone. But, he'd see her in later, unlike the family of the car accident victim, who'd be seeing their relative for the last time in a morgue.

Chapter Eleven

Instinct told Heather she was in a hospital. After she thanked God for sparing her life, she wanted to get up and go home. The world's worst headache was pounding at her. And, she couldn't open her eyes. She figured it was temporary like the time she had her wisdom teeth removed and it took her a while to get reoriented. She wasn't worried. Especially, since she could hear comforting, familiar voices.

"Heather. Darling, you're going to be fine."

Mom. She could smell her perfume. Chanel. She hadn't seen her in awhile and wondered who'd called her.

"Hang in there, kid."

Dad. The last time she'd seen him, he had his checkbook out. She'd rejected his offer, citing she'd make it on her own. But, she'd really screwed things up this time. He'd never forgive her, of that she was sure.

Where's Robbie? Alive, she prayed. What about the baby? Surely, it hadn't survived. Now, a thing of the past, just like she'd wanted, except now having come so close to death, she'd changed her mind. She wanted a baby to love and care for. If only she could go back in time.

Tears formed in her closed eyes, caressing her check. A contrast in anatomy. The warm tears brought on by an overwhelming cold emptiness inside of her. "What happened?" she whispered. Reaching her hand up, wiping the tears, then opening her eyes.

"You were in an accident, but you're going to be fine." A man, she presumed a doctor, stood over her, looking serious and impressive, a stethoscope wrapped around his neck.

"Thank you, Jesus," Robbie said, looking upward. Then, he leaned down to give her a kiss on the cheek, a broad smile of relief crossing his face. He adjusted the crutches under his arms and wondered if it was time for him to take another Vicodan. The cast on his leg seemed to be tightening with each passing hour.

"How long have I been out?" Had it been hours? Days? Weeks?

"Not long at all," the doctor assured her. "As a medical professional, I don't like to use the term, miracle, but let's just say, it was miraculous."

"Could've been worse. The car's totaled. At first look, the paramedics thought you were dead inside the crumpled metal. It looked worse than it was. You're fine. Everyone is fine. That's all that matters."

"That's right, Robbie," said Heather's mother, who'd met Robbie for the first time in the emergency room. The jury was still out in her mind as to whether or not she liked this character. He'd almost killed her daughter, but she was so relieved that Heather was still alive.

"How did you know I was here?"

"Heather, dear, the hospital called us."

"My head hurts."

"You have a concussion," the doctor explained. "And, a few bumps and bruises. You need to stay in the hospital overnight for observation."

What Heather really wanted to ask about was the baby. But, she didn't want to talk about that in front of her parents. Plus, she feared her tears would be endless. She'd never be able to get out of bed. "Who called you?"

"They pulled your purse from the wreckage. We're in your address book."

"Of course."

The doctor interjected, "She needs her rest now."

Her mother kissed her on her forehead, her father on her cheek, and Robbie kissed her on her lips. Then they left the room, the doctor remained.

"I want to talk to you about your pregnancy," the doctor said.

Heather knew what was coming, but she didn't want to

hear it. "It's okay, you don't have to tell me. I already know."

"That the pregnancy is intact?"

"What?" She was confused. Maybe she didn't hear him right.

"Like I said, miraculous."

With the IV tubing trailing, she pulled herself into an upright position. A feat moments before, she'd deemed impossible.

"Are you sure?"

"You'll need to have your pregnancy followed closely, of course."

"Of course."

"I've got to finish my rounds, but I'll be back later. We'll get you out of here in no time," he added with a wink.

"Thank you." Heather's head fell back into the pillow. At that moment, she felt as if she'd just grown up. Closing her eyes, she thought of names for the baby before falling asleep.

When she awoke, she could see through the closed blinds that it was dark outside. Could it be nighttime already? Glancing up at the wall clock, it read two o'clock. She looked over and saw Robbie asleep in a chair next to the bed, his cast propped up on another chair. She figured he'd snuck back into the room. Or talked his way into the nurses letting him stay. She decided to wake him.

Leaning out of the bed, she poked his shoulder. "Robbie, wake up."

"What?" The pain pills made him groggy. "You okay? Need something?"

"I'm more than okay. I'm going to have a baby."

He sat up, and his crutches fell to the ground. Even though it was the middle of the night, he was now fully awake.

"Correction," he said. "We're going to have a baby."

Chapter Twelve

Lucky felt as if something was pinning him down. Was he shackled and exposed on piercing springs of a mold-infested mattress? His aching legs trembled as he tried to break free. His breathing was labored, in need of oxygen. If he wasn't free soon, he would die. That he was sure of. He could feel the perspiration dripping, drop by drop down his innocent face. In the darkness, he only saw space. A void. Praying someone would hear the anguished pleas of a little boy, he cried out. His voice echoed through the black air.

"Lucky, wake up!" J.J. said, grabbing his thrashing shoulders.

"What happened?" His thoughts were confused and disoriented. He sat up, and wiped his groggy, moist eyes. Naked, yet he was burning up. Fever, maybe? Throwing off the heavy bedspread that weighed down his feet, he gasped for air.

"You had a nightmare," J.J. explained, rubbing his sweating back with the palm of her hand.

"Don't." Jerking away, he didn't want to be there. He'd made a horrible mistake and was going to ask for forgiveness.

"I gotta get some air," he said, grabbing a pair of Santa Rita University sweat pants, her alma mater. They were the first thing he found in the bathroom where he ran the faucet and splashed cold water on his face. Putting on a matching sweatshirt, he glimpsed himself in the mirror. He felt, with the collegiate outfit, he had the appearance Heather had wanted, but that J.J. had achieved. Too preppy for him, but at three-thirty in the morning, he couldn't have cared less. On the way into the kitchen, he finger brushed his hair, then slipped on an old pair of running shoes he'd had since New York, discarding the idea of socks.

In the kitchen, he grabbed the car keys and an ice-cold bottle of water. He went out the front door, the cat followed on his heels. A spy. Just what he needed. The cat inched closer to his leg, opened its mouth, hissed, and promptly bit his ankle with its sharp, menacing teeth.

"You bloody cat," he said, reaching down to grab the fast-moving predator. The cat got away just as Lucky's fingertips grazed her fur.

Lucky went into the garage, opened the door, started the car, and backed out. As he neared the end of the steep driveway, he glanced back toward the house. He could see a flickering candle up on the terrace off the master bedroom suite. She'd lit it earlier in the evening when they were watching the sunset. Rolling down the car window, he heard a cat's mournful cry in the distance.

Lucky realized he'd forgotten his cigarettes. "Screw it," he said. Not worth going back.

Chapter Thirteen

Robbie took a taxi to Gabe's downtown office. Gabriel had been asleep when he arrived home from the hospital in the early hours of the morning and had already left for work when Robbie awoke. Not wanting to tell him the good news by phone or e-mail, Robbie went to deliver the communication in person.

On crutches and souped-up on Vicodan, he hobbled out of the cab to the inside of the towering building. The massive piece of granite and glass cast a shadow on the street below. He nodded to a guard who was sitting watch over the incoming and outgoing, hurried folks about the lobby, lemmings going nowhere.

Robbie took the elevator to the twentieth floor and was greeted by an illustrious lobby, filled with potted plants and gilded walls. The gilded walls added a Hollywood touch. The floors were so shiny, they looked as if they'd just been damp mopped.

"Is Gabriel Fuentes in?"

The receptionist peered out from behind that week's copy of a tabloid. "Who?"

"Gabriel Fuentes."

"Do you have an appointment?" With security concerns, of course, she couldn't just let anyone in.

"Can you just check for a guy on crutches?"

She looked up Gabriel's phone extension, buzzed it, but there was no answer. "Sorry. He's not in."

Robbie was sure he was there. He knew Gabe had said he had a big case to work on. "Can't you just let me in?"

"I can't. I could get fired."

"I doubt that."

"You need authorization to be let inside."

"I'm Gabriel's partner. Is that authorization enough?"

"I'm assuming you don't mean law partner?"

Was she trying to be funny? "I've got news that has to be delivered in person."

"I don't—" Her phone rang. She hated it when it became busy, which was all the time. "Bender, Baines and Harwood. Please hold." Never a moment's rest. Reaching into the desk drawer, she thought she'd never finish the magazine.

"Here's a guest badge. Fill in your name, and clip it to your shirt."

"Thanks, I won't be long."

She pressed the all-powerful button, unlocking the door that granted entrance privileges.

Glancing around, Robbie noticed views of the bay that were postcard perfect. Today was one of those gorgeous San Francisco days that songs were written about.

Robbie snuck up to Gabriel and put his hands over his eyes. "Guess who?" he asked, disguising his voice.

"I don't like games," Gabe said, turning around. Surprised to see Robbie, he asked him what he was doing there.

"Just wanted to talk."

"Let me guess. About Heather? Could we discuss this later?"

"I have something to tell you, or ask you."

"She's going to be fine. Don't worry about being sued. Heather's not going to do that."

"I feel responsible for her accident. I want to help . . . with the kid."

"One thing has nothing to do with the other."

"You know how we've talked about adopting a kid?"

Shit. Gabriel had so much work to do, but he had his priorities, too. "Sit down. Let's talk about this rationally." As much as he was sure he and Robbie wanted to adopt someday, that was way down the road. He still had law school to finish.

"You don't want to adopt Heather's baby, do you?" What was Robbie thinking? Was everyone in this city injudicious?

Chapter Fourteen

Lucky found Bender, Baines and Harwood's office easy enough. He knew J.J.'s friend from the restaurant, Gloria, was an attorney, and locating her would be a breeze.

After he'd walked out on J.J. in the middle of the night, he just drove around and in the morning decided to go and see the lawyer. If he was going to get things right with Heather, he had to get things right with his life. He'd just made one stop at a clothing shop along the way and purchased some new clothes, charging them with J.J.'s credit card, wearing them out of the store.

Arriving at the law offices, he just needed to get past the security desk. "I'm from Miss Jones' office. From Nomadic Software. Here to see Gloria Harwood."

"Is she expecting you?"

"No, but she'll see me."

"She doesn't see anyone without an appointment."

"Tell her it's Lucky. And it's urgent."

She phoned Miss Harwood's office and talked with Celia, her assistant.

"Lucky, huh? I heard about him from my friend Abby. Is he as cute as she said?"

"Affirmative."

"Send him up. Miss Harwood's on the phone, but she'll be done soon. And I'll screen him."

"Thanks, doll," he said as he took the badge. Riding the elevator up, he rehearsed what he was going to say to her. First, he'd confess his sins. Then, he'd ask for clemency. Criminals did that all the time.

Janie in the Nomadic Human Resources office had wanted him to provide a passport and birth certificate for tax purposes. He didn't even have a driver's license. He had no choice, but to come clean about his abhorrent past. Starting

with the murder of his father. Self-defense. They'd understand that. Nothing would ever come of it, him being in
another country and all. He knew Gloria could help him with
his immigration papers. She had to. He was ready to move
forward in his life. The secrets needed to be behind him. Stop
running. His night terrors would end, his future begin.

Getting off the elevator, he was stunned. Robbie. He
hadn't seen him since that day he left the restaurant. What
was he doing here? He seemed to be deep in conversation
with someone. Sneaking up behind a neighboring cubicle,
without them noticing, he crouched to listen.

"So, you think you're ready to be a father?"

"I'm going to make a great dad."

Lucky burst out laughing.

Robbie glanced up. "What are you doing here?"

"What are you doing here?" Lucky mocked.

"We're having a private conversation." Robbie's blood
boiled. After what Heather had just been through, it was all
Lucky's fault. Robbie lunged for Lucky's neck.

Gabriel intervened. "Robbie, what are you doing?"

"Leave me alone," Robbie said, as he punched Lucky in
the face, something he'd wanted to do for a long time.

Lucky was stunned. "What's the matter with you? I
could kill you if I wanted to. Besides, what's your problem? I
didn't do anything!"

Robbie glanced around, noticing a crowd had gathered.
"You've done more than you know."

"What is that supposed to mean?"

"Just get the hell out of here, man," Gabriel said, noticing an approaching security guard. He was only an intern, and
he didn't want to lose any opportunity he had for advancement with the firm.

Lucky, walked away. He could've beaten the crap out of
Robbie, but he tried to put the incident out of his mind
instead. He had business, real business, to take care of.
Following the directions to Gloria's office that he'd been

given by someone on the elevator, he neared it, snickering. Thought he had problems. Robbie was more of a kook than he'd realized.

"Everything okay?" the guard asked Gabriel.

"Just a minor misunderstanding. Nothing to be concerned about. You know these custody disputes." He rolled his eyes. "Everything's fine now."

Gabriel patted Robbie on the shoulder. "I think you better go."

"Yeah, okay. I'll see you later." As much as Robbie hated Lucky, he knew the baby would be one gorgeous child.

Chapter Fifteen

Lucky flashed his million-dollar grin at Gloria's assistant. "Is she ready for me?"

"Miss Harwood is unavailable right now."

"It's a matter of the utmost importance."

This guy was smooth, there was no doubting that. "Right, but the thing is, I don't have you on her calendar."

"No, you wouldn't, now would you? But I'm pretty sure Miss Harwood will see me."

He was even more attractive than she'd heard. Word traveled fast when J.J. hired a new stud. "She's on the phone. You'll have to wait."

"No problem." Granted, she was one pretty girl, but he was still thinking about what just transpired with Robbie. Rubbing his neck, he sat down and waited. With time to think, he couldn't help but remember Robbie's comment. Doing more than you know.

Behind the closed door in her office, Gloria was taking in the conversation. "So, he disappeared in the middle of the night?"

"Just like that," J.J. said, confused by Lucky's leaving. He was gone when she woke up and so was the new car she'd just acquired for him.

"Maybe, he's sold the Porsche, took the cash, and went back to his country."

"You think?"

"I'm just kidding. I'm sure he'll turn up. Probably when you'll least expect him."

"I hope you're right," J.J. said as she took the opportunity to search her purse, briefcase and desk for any more stray Xanax pills. If she couldn't find any, she'd have to make that emergency visit to Dr. Wells. The annoying pharmacist refused to refill any more of her anti-anxiety medication without the doctor's approval. And Dr. Wells refused to give her any more refills until she went in for a session. A real quagmire.

J.J. was getting pissed. "The strange thing is—"

"Stranger than a stranger missing?" Gloria laughed.

"This is serious." J.J. found one pill, albeit lint-covered, but it was her savior.

"Okay, sorry. What is it?"

"My cat is missing, too."

"I don't think they do a missing person's report for cats," Gloria said, stifling a laugh. All her cases should be so easy.

J.J. lifted a Nomadic Software mug to her lips and swallowed the pill. The now cold sludge that tried to pass for coffee disgusted her, but she wasn't sure what made her most upset. The thought of Lucky leaving, or the idea that she was being ridiculed — by her best friend, no less.

"I warned you, J.J., not to get involved with him."

"Maybe I should go to the restaurant?"

"Chez Von?"

"Of course." J.J.'s stomach felt as if it had an open wound from the gut-wrenching coffee.

"Forget about the male species for a moment, will you. Do you realize your stock offering is almost here?" Sometimes it was hard to separate their friendship from business. If she were going to bill Nomadic for this conversation, which of course, she was, she had to be an attorney first and best friend last.

"Of course, I know the offering is near." Did she think she was an amateur?

"Have all your sound bites ready?" Gloria harped, not missing a beat as she checked out the updated Web site for Nomadic, taking mental notes of changes they should make, even though they already overhauled it. Her brain never stopped working. She was convinced that's what made her such a great lawyer.

"I've been planning this my whole life," J.J. said defensively. "And, yes, we're ready."

*   *   *

"Is she ever going to be free?" Lucky was tired of waiting. A few minutes was too long for him. He'd tired of sitting in the chair, and now paced about.

Ignoring his impatience, Gloria's assistant said she'd be right back. She had to go to the bathroom, but she didn't tell him that.

Lucky was glad she left. He wasted no time.

*   *   *

"You've got to focus on what's at—" Gloria said. Her tone was louder than intended and the realization that someone else was listening from across the room stopped her conversation mid-sentence. Her eyes widened in surprise. "You?"

"What is it?" J.J. asked.

"I'll call you back," Gloria said, hanging up, motioning him to sit.

"Did my assistant let you in, just like that?"

"Well, she had to leave." He wanted to get to the heart of the matter. Not being one to beat around the bushes, he came right out with it. "I'm in trouble."

"Tell me about it." Her eyes narrowed as she was drawn to his dark and mysterious eyes. What was he doing here? How did he find her? Of course, she knew who he was immediately. She'd never forget his stunning looks. As she looked him over in a secret way, she was impressed by whatever deception tactics he used to make it all the way into her private office.

Lucky circled the room once, noticing the unusual art on the walls. "You a collector?"

"Is that what you're here for? To talk to me about art?"

"No, I—" How did he say it?

"While you're thinking about it, in answer to your question. Yes, I am an avid collector with an eye for untapped talent." She smiled.

"Oh?" Was she coming on to him?

"What can I do for you?"

"I'm in trouble," he blurted out, again.

She figured he was. Why else would he be there? Her eagle eyes ran down his body like a slow metal detector. Was that a crust of dried blood on his ankle? Did he have blood on his hands?

Gloria picked up the phone, and called J.J. She should know he was okay, but changed her mind and hung up. She wanted to hear his story first.

She readied herself in her Italian leather chair. Behind her were floor to ceiling windows capturing a view of the Bay Bridge with its nonstop traffic. Cars moved in a determined, steady stream.

"Mr. Lawson, have a seat."

She wished she could smoke in her office, but had quit because it became too difficult. Smokers were banished to outdoor sidewalks, where furrowed eyebrows passed judgment with fake coughs and disapproving glares.

Crossing her legs, she propped a yellow legal-sized pad on her knee, balanced a silver pen in her fingers. This was going to be good, she could feel it in her bones. He wouldn't have come to her otherwise.

"Let's have it."

"I'm in the country illegally."

"Oh?"

"Yes, and I need help with my immigration?"

"Is that all?"

"Isn't that enough?" He had second thoughts about confessing the rest.

Gloria slapped down the note pad onto her desk. "Mr.

Lawson, I have to tell you, I thought you were going to tell me that you'd murdered someone or something." She let out a sigh. "My firm can handle this for you." Though she knew when a client was not being honest with her. Was he kidding? That was it? That was why he ran away? A few pertinent phone calls, some hasty paperwork, and she'd see to it that he was legal. A student visa. Temporary visa. This was easy, too easy. She couldn't help but be disappointed. She knew there was more to this guy's story. He was hiding more behind his secretive eyes than he let on, of that she was certain.

"I'll help you. But, I can only do so if you're honest with me and with yourself."

"I don't know what you want me to say?" Lucky felt as if he were stuttering.

"Is there a girl involved?" Gloria knew about Heather, the beach bunny as J.J. referred to her, confessing that he called out her name in the night.

"No, there's no woman involved."

"I'll help with the temporary residency paperwork and temporary work visa, but my guess is there's more."

Lucky squirmed. What had she known? Did it have something to do with Robbie? Was Robbie going to file some kind of harassment suit against him for something he said to him at Chez Von? Is that why Robbie was there?

"Here's my card, call me anytime. But, also, here's a card of someone you should see. She may be able to help you. I don't mean with legalities, I mean with personal issues."

Jesus, did he have the word murderer branded across his face? What had J.J. told her? "Thanks." Lucky stuffed it into his wallet without looking at it.

"Now, with that out of the way, let's talk immigration issues." .

Later, on his way back to Nomadic, he finally read the other card. "Evelyn Wells, M.D. Board Certified in Psychiatry."

Chapter Sixteen

Driving back to the office, Lucky threw the business card for the psychiatrist out the car window. Had Gloria thought he was nuts? Was it that obvious?

Instead, he pulled into a parking lot. He'd seen the cross from a distance, and it drew him, giving off a certain glow, compelling him to go inside. Was it his denomination? Did he even have one anymore? Didn't matter anyway. He just wanted to look around the intriguing building. Or, so, he convinced himself.

He hadn't been inside a church since his school days. Sister Anne and the other students would go to Mass and confession. Maybe, that's what he needed to do now. Grateful the heavy doors were unlocked, he walked toward the front of the large church. The stained glass windows reflected colors of the rainbow, a breathtaking sight.

Sitting on a hard wooden pew, he felt ten-years-old again, and the prayers that he'd memorized as a child came back. Automatically, he knelt down and recited the rosary, feeling closer to God. He asked for forgiveness, but he'd done so many horrible things in his life that he didn't know where to start. When he finished, he sat back, sensing a person behind him. How long had someone been sitting there? His ten-year-old self heard a scolding voice. Don't turn around in church. But, never did he listen.

"It's okay if I'm here, isn't it?" He didn't know why the words came out of his mouth so polite.

"Of course. I'm sorry if I disturbed you. I didn't mean to."

"No, no. You didn't disturb me. I was just leaving."

"I'm Father Ted." The priest reached out his hand.

"Lucky."

"We always welcome visitors."

"I'm not a visitor. I live here. In California."

"That's not what I meant."

"I didn't think so."

Lucky turned to leave. He'd already wasted enough time. "Nice meeting you."

"Same to you."

Upon leaving the church, he headed to the condo where he showered, changed his clothes, and called J.J. at the office. "I'll be back tomorrow. Just need to do something first."

"I was worried about you. You just disappear like that. What happened?" But, J.J. already knew what happened. Gloria had called her, told her everything.

Gloria had blurted it out, then sworn her to secrecy. They always ended up spilling the beans with each other, from stock secrets to sex secrets. Neither could keep their mouths shut.

But, J.J. just wanted to hear it from Lucky. Him telling her the truth.

"Just some legal stuff. Everything's fine."

"Legal stuff?" Was he going to be honest with her? She hired him to be her assistant, and so far, he'd only assisted himself.

"Don't worry. Gloria's taking care of it."

"My Gloria?" She tried to sound surprised.

"I didn't think you'd mind if I went and saw her. I needed legal advice, and I remembered her from the restaurant."

"And my address book in my computer?"

"That, too."

As mad as she was at him, she couldn't get through it without two things, her pills and Lucky. For the pills, she'd go see Dr. Wells after all, but she couldn't refill this man with a prescription.

Chapter Seventeen

Lucky flew over the hill as if he owned the road. Not bothering to call first, he wanted to surprise Heather.

The duplex was still the same. The pealing stucco needed repairing, cars with surfboard racks lined the street, taking up most of the parking spots. Parking down the block, he jogged up the street. This seemed like old times. Getting out of the car, he breathed in the clean sea air and wished he hadn't missed the sunset.

Ringing the doorbell, he wondered why there was no answer. Probably broken. Knocking now, he wondered why he couldn't see any lights on the inside. She probably had candles. He lifted the geranium pot and took the spare key. Heather would be so pleased to see him, she wouldn't mind if he waited for her. She'd be home soon, never being one to stay out late.

Winslow gave Lucky a slobbery kiss the minute he came through the front door. "Hey, boy. How are yuh doing?" Just now, he'd realized how much he missed the dog, too.

Petting Winslow, Lucky asked, "Where is she, boy? Gonna be home soon?"

The dog ran to his doggie door that led to the backyard and came back in holding a frayed tennis ball in his mouth.

"Okay, fella. Let's look for Heather on the beach." Lucky and Winslow retraced the steps the trio had made many times. How Lucky's heart ached. Heather had only been good and loving to him, and he'd crushed her. Sitting on their bench, the moon lit the ocean as the thought of seeing Heather again lifted his spirits. He'd wait for her even if it took forever.

"Come on, boy, let's go home.'"

At the house, he asked, "Got any beer in the fridge?"

Winslow wagged his tail.

With beer in hand and a longing heart, Lucky sat on the sofa, falling asleep before the first sip. When he opened his eyes, it was morning. The dog was curled up at his feet. Shit. Hadn't she come home? Checking her bedroom and seeing she wasn't there, he decided that waiting all night was long enough. This was a big day. Lucky had to be to the office to witness the initial public offering that was sure to change his life forever. He was an employee of the hottest high-tech company in the valley, all abuzz, and he was a part of it.

After he gave the dog some fresh water, and dog food, he left the duplex, but on his way toward his car, he stopped, turned and glanced back. "I will do better for you, Heather. You'll see."

"She ain't home."

Lucky turned his head. "Oh. Hi, how are you?"

"I'm fine, but she ain't there," Wanda said. She continued watering her roses with a hose, not bothering to look at him directly.

"Don't happen to know where I might find her, do yuh?" He walked toward her.

"I've been taking care of the dog, I'll be right over to feed it."

"I already fed it this morning."

"You broke her heart, you know."

He didn't want to talk about this with Wanda. This was none of her business. "Never mind." Lucky walked toward his car, which was now blocked in by two surfer cars.

"She's in the hospital."

Her voice was faint while he got farther away. What was the old bat trying to say? "What?" Sounded like she said, "hospital" but that couldn't be right. Rubbing his back, it ached from sleeping on the uncomfortable sofa, he returned toward her. "What did you say?"

"She's in the hospital."

"What the fu— I mean, what happened? Is it serious? What happened?"

"She was in a car accident with another fella."

He'd kill the guy. As the thought of killing ran through his mind, Lucky realized that his thoughts were dangerous. After all, he'd killed before, right?

"She's in San Francisco, at Memorial."

"Thanks," he yelled back to her. He was already in his car. Thank God, he had fast wheels.

*   *   *

At the hospital, Lucky pulled into a parking spot marked, CLERGY ONLY. Getting out of the car, it dawned on him that he barely remembered the drive. He was just glad to be there.

"Could you tell me what room Heather Kane is in?" he asked the silver-haired lady, who wore a pink smock.

"Yes, dear," she said, scrolling through names on a computer monitor.

"She was in a car accident." Lucky prayed it wasn't serious.

The lady muttered to herself. "Don't have a Heather Kane. There's a Heather in 301, but it's not Kane."

"Never mind," he said. "I'll find her."

Stopping at the gift shop, he bought a bouquet of white daisies, then headed up to room 301. What were the odds of there being more than one Heather in the hospital? Peering into the room, he saw that it was already filled with flowers. Lots of flowers, and balloons. Where had they all come from? They made his meager offering seem futile.

"Heather?" He tiptoed up to the bed, flowers in hand.

She opened her eyes. She'd only been waiting for the doctor to come in to release her. "Lucky? What are you doing here?"

"I heard about your accident. Are you okay?" Unavoidable tears formed. Heather looked as if the life had been drained out of her. She was gray and thinner.

"I'm fine."

"These are for you." He glanced around. "You have a lot of well-wishers."

She didn't know what to say at first. "I'm just so surprised to see you." She took the flowers. "These are beautiful, thank you."

"Heather, do you mind if I sit down?"

"Of course, not." She thought she'd be angry with him. But, she wasn't. She only felt peace.

"I want to talk to you." He didn't know why he was nervous. All he had to do was tell her that he loved her. He wanted to explain, why he'd left so abruptly. That his past left him paralyzed to make any commitments. The blood in him would never make a good father. He didn't have it in him. He'd be just like his old man.

He stared into her ocean-blue eyes. "Heather, I have something I have to say."

"I have something too."

"Let me talk first, I've been waiting long enough. Heather, I love you." The tears that had been welling fell freely down his cheeks.

She opened her arms in a welcoming gesture. "Come here."

Lucky fell into her open arms. "I'm so sorry," he said.

"It's okay."

They didn't notice when the doctor walked into the room. "Well, are you ready to go home, Heather?"

Tears were swimming in her eyes. She'd come into the hospital with tears of pain, and now she was leaving with tears of joy, a baby on the way, and the man she loved.

"I need to talk to her alone for a few minutes," the doctor said.

"No problem, sir." Lucky didn't take his eyes off Heather.

Nice young man, the doctor thought. Was he the baby's father?

Lucky embraced Heather and their lips, so long apart, found each other again.

"I meant now."

"Oh, right." Lucky stood up. "Heather, I have to make a phone call. Be right back."

"Okay." She was so glad to be going home. But, how would she explain her situation to Lucky?

*   *   *

The doctor examined her again, pronounced her fit, and signed her release papers.

"Will the young man be driving you home, dear?"

"I think so," Heather said, grinning.

*   *   *

Lucky was on the phone in the hallway with J.J. who was at her office. "Babe, I'll be right there." Lucky was so close to the jackpot, he didn't want to blow it with J.J. now. How could he ask Heather to marry him if he didn't have a future? "I have a meeting with Gloria—since I'm already in the city—I'll go there first. Then I need to go to the condo—shower and change. Do you really want to hear all this?"

"Not really."

"And, I have a surprise for you."

After he hung up, he went back into Heather's room. "Something urgent has come up at the office. I'll see you later, at home."

"I guess—"

"Love you," he said, kissing her on the mouth, and left before she could say anything.

Lucky still brought shivers up and down her spine. "Love you, too."

A nurse came into the room. "Your ride is downstairs. I'll take you down in a wheelchair."

"I can walk," Heather insisted.

"Hospital policy."

"You ready, Angel?" her father said, opening the car door for her.

"Am I ever." She smiled at the thought of how a few minutes could change a life. The two men most important in her life, her father and the father of her baby, soon would meet for the first time.

Chapter Eighteen

John Dunn took shit from no one, except his wife Sasha.

"Those bitches! What are you going to do about it?" Sasha ranted, having just returned from a meeting that didn't go the way she expected.

Sasha had John wrapped around her little finger like a noose around a calf's neck. Only the calf was dripping in fear, and Sasha was dripping in diamonds and Ritz Carlton hand lotion.

He was convinced the only shout from the crowd she'd heard was the clapping at the monthly Valley Women's League luncheons when someone else was nominated as Chairman of the Winter Ball. "Darling, it doesn't matter," he tried to reassure her. He could take on anyone, any loose cannon who spent his invested money, but his wife was a wildcat.

"Those women, they hate me," she said, throwing down her Louis Voitton purse, a must have item.

"Calm down, dear," he said, picking up her purse, searching through it for her prescription bottle.

"I'm gonna call them to say that you'll underwrite the whole thing!" she screamed. "Then, they'll have to pick me."

John inwardly chuckled at his recognition of another tantrum. The woman was furious at once again being passed over as belle of the ball. He didn't understand what it was with Valley wives. Why weren't they happy to just play tennis and get their nails done?

"I'm calling Brianna right now," she said, reaching for the phone.

Why did wives have to spend their days planning parties disguised as charity events? Events that were funded by their husbands who were dragged there kicking and screaming. Of course, nothing but unbearable tuxedos could they be clad in. The rubber-like chicken and watered down drinks were another bonus. All the while, the women gushed at how beautiful they each were in their beaded dresses, and trashed each other the minute their backs were turned.

John didn't have time for this kind of nonsense. When he was back home in Texas, his sainted mother used to ride alongside the raunchy men on their cattle ranch. Then she'd go into the kitchen that decorated with yellow checkered curtains and cook up a batch of her county fair award winning fried chicken and corn bread biscuits. The food smelled of heaven and tasted divine. She'd never complained, not her whole life. Not when her husband, John's father, left them. Not even on her death bed.

Holding a glass of lemonade with a slice of lime, John went out to the redwood deck overlooking the valley. On a TV built into the glass top of his patio table, just like a place mat, he watched the business report. Anticipation was building. There was nothing like offering day. His latest baby, Nomadic, was going to be an IPO destined for the stratosphere. The stocks were garnering a great buzz, and he could feel it in his Texan blood.

He could also feel the noose tightening around his neck, and his wife held the rope. He'd authorize a sizable check for the Valley Women's League, benefitting God only knew what charity. John Dunn, the most powerful V. C. in the valley, was putty in his wife's hands.

Chapter Nineteen

Lucky walked into J.J.'s office, transformed. His face looked as if he'd been on vacation, but his body was dressed for success. He was paving his way for success, not just for himself, but for Heather, too. And, the big day had arrived. The timing of joining Nomadic couldn't have been better. The excitement that was in the air could be felt the minute he walked into the building.

"There you are." J.J. tried not to look as pissed as she felt. "Where've you been?"

"Had a few things to take care of." He had to play his cards right, not wanting to alienate her. This was a tightrope he was walking and he wanted the riches that waited for him at the other side.

"Gloria told me everything."

"Is she allowed to do that?"

Throwing her head back, she laughed. "You have so much to learn."

Lucky ignored that remark, nothing was going to bother him today. The game had begun, the ball was in motion, and he was the quarterback with a golden future. Putting his arms around her, he swept her off her feet, and swung her around. "This is the big day, huh?"

Lucky looked good. Was it his hair that had changed? There was something different about him. Maybe it was his new attire. He seemed to have matured into a high-tech chic. "So glad you could make it," she said. "But please put me down." But, she loved it when their bodies touched. Like a smoldering fire that would erupt at any minute.

"Come on, babe, I've got options, too, you know."

"You could hardly compare what you have to what I have as company president." What he had was a joke compared to hers.

"Don't spoil it for me." He kissed her on the cheek.

She didn't forgive that easily. And she was curious about his laissez-faire attitude. There was one thing that hadn't changed, his mysterious eyes calling out to her and that wicked smile.

"I don't need you as an assistant anymore," she lied.

He laughed. "Like you ever did? We both know what you wanted from me."

"I don't know what you're talking about."

"Is this room bugged or something? Afraid of the Board of Directors?"

"Don't be ridiculous." Maybe it was bugged? She'd better have it checked out.

"I brought you a present." He hadn't planned on giving it to J.J. but, decided to tease her.

"Oh? Diamonds charged on my account?"

"Nothing like that," he said, handing her a yellow bag. "I hope you're not disappointed."

"What's this?" she asked, sniffing into the bag. "Smells like peanut butter."

"It is, but it's taffy."

"Taffy?"

"That's right. Salt water."

"You're kidding, right?" She walked over to a table, where an assortment of real gifts were. Overflowing fruit baskets, flowers, plants, Godiva chocolates. She tossed the bag. "That was so generous of you." She removed a card from the largest gift basket, and put it into her desk drawer, planning on having it framed.

He laughed as she spoke. "That's not my real gift." He handed her an envelope.

Glancing inside, she knew what it was. Gloria had already told her. He was legal. At least for now. Even had a temporary driver's license. He wasn't going to blow his future by not providing the proper paperwork.

"Gloria works quick."

"Guess that's what she gets the big bucks for. By the way, you'll be getting her bill," Lucky said.

Taking his hand into hers, she seductively pulled him toward her. "I think there's a better position for you here at the company." Why did her deepest desires fill with lust toward this guy? Why couldn't she just let him go? He'd make money through the offering; get what he wanted. But, she couldn't let him out of her life. Surely another guy could be found who was cut from the same cloth as herself.

"Tell me about this new position." After all, two could play this game.

"It's not what you think." She walked over to him, and put her hands around his waist. "There's room for you in Sales," she offered, standing on her tiptoes to kiss him. He was so much taller than she. "There's always room in Sales."

Chapter Twenty

"I just have one stop, Daddy," Heather said, as they left the hospital. She wore a clinging, ribbed T-shirt with a heart on the front in gold rivets. Her faded blue jeans had holes in the knees. A fringe hung down from the waist. She was barely able to button the front. They were too tight. Soon she'd have to trade them in for maternity clothes. Her red suede cowboy boots still fit her like slippers.

A smile dressed her lips when she thought how Lucky had come to her. He'd left in such a hurry, she didn't get a chance to tell him that he was going to be a father. She was too impatient to wait until later that day. Plus, she knew he'd want to know right away. Would he be as excited as she was? She was going to have their baby.

"You look beautiful," her father said. Of course, she was his little angel. He'd always loved her and was sorry they had had a falling out. About what the argument was, he couldn't remember. She just walked out of the house one day, determined to make it on her own. After she graduated from a private high school, they wanted her to go to a small, private university where she'd be more protected. Eligible, appropriate suitors would have been at her disposal. But, she was strong-headed and stubborn just like he was. Now, he wanted to be the father that he never had time to be before. He also wanted to be the grandfather that he'd always dreamed of being.

"Could I just ask you something, darling?"

"Of course."

"How could you think your mother and I wouldn't have been delighted to have a grandchild?"

"Well—" Did he really want to get into all that now?

Sensing her uncomfortable vibes, he realized there was plenty of time to talk.

"Where do you want to stop?" he asked. "To get your dog?" He hoped that wasn't the case, but was willing to make the sacrifice of having the mutt around. He would just instruct the staff to make sure and clean up after it.

"No, Dad, I'll get him myself later. In the meantime, my neighbor has been taking care of him for me." She'd planned on staying with her parents for a few days before going home.

Opening the car window, she wanted to feel the breeze flow through her hair. She ran her finger through the length. Soon she would have it cut. Putting her boots up on the back of the front seat, she stretched her legs, tired of being cooped up in the hospital. Going out for a long walk was an event she looked forward to. Her heavy heart was now at peace. Lucky was back.

"Heather, I'm sorry for everything in the past." How painful it was for him. Dr. Wells' words were powerful, encouraging her father to be open with his feelings toward Heather. Now that she was back in his life, perhaps they'd all go in for therapy. Dr. Wells would approve.

"I'll tell you when to get off the freeway," Heather said. "Just drive like we're going to your house."

"Our house."

"Our house."

They drove south, out of the city, heading down the peninsula.

"Get off at the next exit," she said. "I called ahead for directions since I didn't have my computer with me at the hospital. Besides, Internet directions are sometimes wrong."

"Looks like we're going to Nomadic Software?" Heather's father asked.

"That's right."

He wondered if J.J. had received the gift he had his assistant send. Not even sure what it was, he'd just told his assistant to send something nice, a good luck token. But, more than that, he wondered how much of a return he'd get on the seed money he'd put into Nomadic.

The parking lot was full.

"Let me out in the front," Heather said.

She wasn't surprised when Jean-Marc had filled her in on where and who Lucky was working for when she'd gone in to quit. Lucky had wasted no time going to the restaurant in his new Porsche to show off and brag about his new job. Jean-Marc wasted no time in filling Heather in on what a rotten person he was.

"I'm looking for Lucky Lukovich," Heather said.

The receptionist inside the front lobby looked at her with disdain. It was going to be a long day, and she couldn't wait till her shift ended so she could join the inevitable party.

"We don't have a Lucky Lukovich employed here." She must've known every employee, and he wasn't one of them.

"Of course, you do." She didn't want to mention the boss' name, but did. "He works for Jennifer Jones." There the words were out. First thing Lucky would have to do is quit his job here. He could work for her father.

"Who are you looking for?"

"I'm looking for Mr. Lukovich. He works for Jennifer Jones. I think you know who she is?"

What was with this young cowgirl? Her clothing gave a new definition to the phrase casual business attire. "Is she expecting you?" She waved in a crew of caterers with trays of king crab legs and sushi.

"I don't want to see her, but it's important that I speak to her assistant." Heather fidgeted in her boots. Her feet were sweating and felt swollen. "She'll know where he is." Not for long.

"They're in a meeting," the receptionist said, sipping champagne. She was already feeling tipsy and wondered if it were too soon to call it a day. "Unless you're with the press, I can't let you in."

"Oh," Heather said, slapping her hand onto the desk. "Did I forget to mention that I'm with the Sea Breeze Gazette?"

"Yes, you did forget," she said, not really believing her. But it had been such a crazy day with the offering and all, she wasn't sure who all had been let in and who hadn't. "Show me your credentials." She took another sip of the bubbly.

"Sure thing," Heather said, searching through her purse. She was glad that she'd gotten everything replaced so fast that had been in her purse during the accident. Pulling out a credit card, she flashed it for a second.

"Okay. Sign in here." The receptionist pointed to an elevator. "Go up to the seventh floor. You can ask for directions from there."

"Right," Heather said, tossing her American Express Platinum Card back into her purse.

On the seventh floor, activity level was high. People were chatting at a high decibel level and running around everywhere. TV sets were tuned to a business channel, and balloons and trays of food abounded. Bottles of champagne and soda filled one long table, and displayed was a sign that read, "We Did It!"

Someone directed her to the office, but the desk she presumed to be Lucky's was vacant. She knocked on the closed door that read, "President," and underneath, "Jennifer Jones."

Maybe Lucky was in her office. She just wanted a peek at the man-stealer. Heather wasn't a bit nervous. After all, she was having his baby. A fact, she couldn't wait to share with him.

There was no answer, but hearing voices inside, she knocked again. No response. Everyone around seemed to be preoccupied. Lucky had a right to know. Now, that they were going to be back together, they had their future to plan. The sooner he got away from here, the better. He could come back home with her to discuss with her father, his options. Not stock options, but life options.

Anxious to see him, she decided to walk into the office. Perhaps the seducer Ms. Jones was on the phone and couldn't answer the door, herself. Slowly, Heather stepped in and saw her, embraced in a passionate kiss. "Oh, my God."

"What do you want?" J.J. shouted. "This is a private office."

"Heather, what are you doing here?" Lucky said, instinctively wiping his lips.

"Oh, this just figures," Heather said.

"It's not what you think."

"Don't even try and say that. I don't care what you say. And to think, I'd thought you'd changed."

"Heather, it's not like that."

"Right."

"What did you want, anyway?"

"Nothing. I didn't want anything. That's not true, there is something."

"Yeah?"

"I don't want to see you ever again!" She turned around and ran out. With a lump in her throat, and tears harboring, she ran passed a group of people who looked as if they were having their own party.

"Hey, join us," someone said, half-drunk. Someone else shoved a glass of champagne into her face. "Party—"

"I don't think so," she said. What stupid idiots.

"Come on," some man said, grabbing her arm, "We're all gonna be millionaires. Billionaires."

"I already am, asshole!" she said, jerking away from him, leaving him with a rejected look.

*   *   *

"See what you've done," Lucky said to J.J.

"Me? I think you've got that backwards. Keep your priorities straight, young man. You're the one that came to me looking for gold, remember?"

Lucky defiantly stared at her. She was busy brushing her

hair and putting on lipstick for her victory speech to the troops. How could she be so callous? He had to go after Heather. Her coming into the office had been such a blur, her golden locks flying behind her when she turned around and left.

"Don't even think about it," J.J. said, reading his mind. "It's either me or the beach bunny. You're in the big league now. Where money, not sand, means something."

"I'll be back," he said, running out of the office after Heather.

"When you come back, bring me coffee. Hazelnut, not Turkish."

She needed her head clear while being congratulated for heading up the highest IPO of the year. She wondered if John Dunn had called yet. The time had come for her to propose her next idea.

A caravan of trucks were parked outside of Nomadic. Catering trucks working the celebration, news vans with their high antennas sticking into the air, reporters running around getting sound bites, and cameramen following, recording prosperity in progress.

*   *   *

"Let's go," Heather said, fighting tears as she jumped into the back seat.

"Okay, angel." Her father nodded to the chauffeur.

*   *   *

Lucky searched the parking lot, in vain, his eyes roving like a lifeguard on lookout duty, but she and her car were nowhere to be seen. How could she have disappeared so fast? Glancing up at the building, he saw J.J. at the window staring at him. He was going to have to lay the law down as he saw it.

He went back upstairs, deciding to explain to Heather later. Today was when his future began. He planned to cement it.

J.J. had her speech in her hand. "Where's the coffee?"

"Get yourself another servant," Lucky said.

"Come here, darlin'." She reached for his hand and nodded out the window. "Take a look."

He refused her hand, but walked to the window.

"Take a good hard look baby. The valley. The money. The power. It's what you want. What you came here for. Not vapor, something that doesn't really exist; something you pretend is there, only isn't."

                    *   *   *

Down the freeway, the white Rolls Royce, with "SANGER 1" license plates headed home.

"It's going to be okay," her father said.

"It's over," Heather said. If only she hadn't been in such an emotional state, maybe she'd be able to stop crying.

Billy Sanger leaned over and put his arm around his daughter to comfort her. How he hated to see her upset. "No, angel," he said. "It's only the beginning."

Part Two

Chapter Twenty One

Heather, nearly nine-months pregnant, sat beneath the shade of a hundred-year-old elm tree at the Sanger estate in Atherton. The wispy branches filled with delicate leaves so low they almost touched her easel. She dipped the tip of the brush into the paint, using sweeping strokes, bringing forth the beauty of her vision. Carried away, she failed to fully notice the lady standing behind her.

"There's a phone call for you, ma'am. A Mr. Robert Barnes, calling from New York." The maid handed Heather the phone that was on a silver tray. A glass of milk and plate of oatmeal cookies waited for Heather on a nearby table.

"Robbie? Can you hang on for just a sec—?"

"Sure."

Heather smiled at the maid. "Thank you, Doreen. That'll be all."

"Yes, ma'am. Before I go in, Mrs. Sanger wanted to remind you that she's having her meeting inside."

"I know. Tell her I'll stay out of the way," Heather said, rolling her eyes in a mock-disgusted manner, then smiling.

Heather put the phone back to her ear. "Robbie, are you still there?"

"Yeah. What's going on?" He glanced at all the trash in the midtown New York flat he was sharing with another actor. Food take-out containers abounded, all empty and molding.

"Just the usual billionaire social scene."

Robbie laughed. "My darling, how could you have kept that secret from me for so long? Billy Sanger's daughter. Fledging college student. All along, an heiress in disguise." Though angry at first for not telling him from the beginning, he'd forgiven her. She was still his barefoot girl, his dearest friend.

"I would've told you sooner or later. The accident and

the baby have brought my parents and me back together."

"Is that good or bad?"

"So far, definitely good."

"I only have a few minutes, Heather, I'm between rehearsals. By the way, thank you for whatever you did to get the wheels moving on my acting career."

"You did it with your talent." Heather had her father make a single phone call which resulted in an audition for a part in a Broadway play. Robbie did the rest.

"How can I ever thank you?"

"By being my baby's Godfather, of course."

"Without question."

"Been going out much, Robbie?"

"Don't have much time for that, you know the theater has killer hours. After work, it's late. Sometimes I go out."

"So, it's not all work?"

"Not all the time. Tonight we're going out, it's Brad's birthday."

"Brad?"

"Don't get any ideas. This guy is straight. The place we're going to is a strip club, if you can believe that?"

"Sounds entertaining." The only entertainment Heather had lately was watching reruns of her baby's sonogram. But, that was okay. "Which club are you going to?" The only New York strip club Heather had ever heard of was Scores.

"The place has some goofy name. Quirks or something."

Petting Winslow, Heather thought he rubbed against her leg more like a cat than a dog. Laughing, she felt a twinge inside. "It's called what?"

"I remember now, Corky's."

Chapter Twenty Two

Talking to Robbie in New York brought home how much she missed him. How much she loved him. She and her mother had been getting along better, but there was nothing like a best friend and that was Robbie personified.

Her mother had been trying, even attended pregnancy classes with her. To this day, there was one thing Heather puzzled about. Why was her mother so involved with committees and all the meetings that went along with them? But they were good causes and seemed to bring her mother happiness. She even seemed to thrive on all the bickering that ping-ponged amongst the ladies.

During Heather's last trimester, she spent more time at her parents' palatial estate, and less time in Sea Breeze. A need to be near family was strong as she prepared for the birth of her child.

Her parents had been so great, so caring, and understanding. Her father said nothing when she brought Winslow to the mansion. The dog delighted in running through the house with the maids chasing him. Trying to keep him off the furniture was a full time job in itself.

The day Heather had mentioned in passing to her father that she was interested in painting, she soon found a room inside the estate converted into an art studio. The place was filled to the brim with supplies.

The Sanger estate was known as Villa de Santiago. And had been rebuilt and refurbished to resemble a Mediterranean villa where the Sangers had once vacationed. Billy had the marble and stone brought over piece-by-piece, and reset to recreate the exact palace that his wife wanted.

They had bought the land on the mid-peninsula years ago for a bundle of cash, demolished the existing house, and built what the land commanded. A fine estate worthy of the area.

Billy quit keeping tabs on the construction, pocket change to him. His fortune just kept growing every year. Being one of the wealthiest men in the world wasn't fun if he had to count every dime. That's what he paid his accountants and lawyers for. He'd rather spend his time on a recreated villa, relaxing on the balcony. This was the perfect view to watch his soon-to-be born grandchild run and play. The acreage was park-like with lush and expansive gardens. To him this was an ideal setting for that grandchild, who would inherit a portion of this one day, after all.

*   *   *

Inside the mansion, Patrice Sanger's meeting was well underway. The outgoing Executive Board of the Women's League was there, dreading the announcement that Brianna Montgomery, the president of the Board was about to make.

"And so, it is with great pleasure that we elect Sasha Dunn as chairman of this year's Winter Ball," Brianna said.

"Here, here," Patrice said, gritting her teeth. She knew they were in for a year of hell with Sasha at the helm of the Ball committee.

"Oh, thank you," Sasha said. Her face beamed with pride.

The twelve board members smiled and clapped politely as the woman they felt was completely wrong for the task was voted in unanimously. She was disorganized and rude, never holding meetings on time or in an orderly manner. The woman didn't even know how to make an agenda.

She would never really fit in, or be one of the group, but with her generous husband underwriting as much as he did, there was no other choice. None of the other husbands were willing to part with as much money as John Dunn, not even Billy Sanger.

Unbeknownst to Sasha, the women had taken their own secret vote. They had all agreed, the following year to oust the bitch. And, her reign hadn't even yet begun.

*   *   *

"Shit," Gloria said, racing down the long tree lined driveway. "Late for the stupid meeting." She hit the brakes, coming to an abrupt stop, her headlights flashed against a row of bushes. "What is this?" She opened the window and peered out to figure out if she'd taken a wrong turn.

"You may enter now, Miss Harwood." A low, masculine voice seemed to come from the trees. The row of green, thick brush opened, revealing that it was in fact an iron gate in disguise.

"Thank you," she shouted out the window, knowing full well she was being monitored from hidden cameras recording her every move.

When she drove through the gate, she could see ahead to the Sanger mansion. She wondered if she had driven too far south, ending up at the Hearst Castle. She had heard through the valley gossip mill how they spent years and millions building the brand new estate, only to make it look old. A three-story villa that looked as if it were home to royalty. But then Sanger was royalty. Gloria couldn't wait to get a glimpse of this king's life.

As she drove closer to the main house, she was amazed by the massive fountains with cascading water that emerged from a pond. This was a perfect decoration for the front of the estate. The fountains made the one at her house seem like a kindergarten project. She could just make out the end of the tennis courts down a hill, behind some cottages that were the size of most people's homes. She couldn't see it, but she heard that somewhere on the property was a gym, complete with indoor basketball court and swimming pool with a retractable roof. Down another hillside were vineyards, a must for any California property that had more than a half-acre, and the Sanger property qualified as a winery.

Nearing the house, Gloria saw a young man wearing a red bow tie over a white shirt, waving her in. Coming to a stop, she glanced over and saw at least a ten-car garage. Was that his mother-of-pearl Rolls? How she'd love to go for a spin in that car. The young guy smiled at her.

"I'll take it from here, ma'am." Opening her car door, his smile grew.

"Thanks, doll." Barely glancing at him, she tried to take in the ambiance of the estate and all its glory, wondering where she had gone wrong in her life.

"Am I too late?" Gloria asked, as an astute looking gentleman with an English accent answered the door.

"They are in the solarium, Miss Harwood," he said in a low, gravely voice. "Do you know where it is?"

"Yes, of course," she lied. Of course, she had no idea where the solarium was, but she didn't want to admit to the hired help that she'd never been to the Sanger estate. That would have been more embarrassing than the time she walked into court with toilet paper stuck to her shoe.

Walking down the long hallway, she wondered if, in fact, she was at a museum.

Seeing sunlight streaming out of a doorway, she assumed it was the solarium. Entering the room, she saw paintings, some finished, others, art in progress, and enough art supplies to open a supply store. This was no solarium. Intrigued, she walked in, glad that she had volunteered her time and legal expertise. Though she'd never been to a meeting, she had been serving as advisor for the Valley Women's League for several years.

When it was Mrs. Sanger's turn to host a meeting, and when the socialite decided to host the splash out of her own house instead of at the country club, Gloria couldn't pass up the rare opportunity. Maybe she'd even accidentally get lost in the mansion and just happen to bump into him. Meeting the reclusive Billy Sanger would make coming to the petty gathering worthwhile.

"Can I help you?" Heather asked, to the woman who was trespassing in her private, off limits to everyone room. "Hello?" Was the woman deaf? Why didn't she answer?

Gloria could not take her eyes off of the painting on the wall and almost forgotten about the meeting. What were the chances of bumping into King Sanger, anyhow? With her artistic eyes, Gloria analyzed the portrait of the subject that captivated her. A woman with delicate features whose auburn hair fell loosely down her long neck wore a mysterious white flower tucked in an alluring manner behind her ear. Her creamy skin glowed. But there was something about her eyes. Something that rang familiarity in the seductive way the eyes in the portrait communicated.

"I have to have this."

"I beg your pardon?"

"I have to have this painting."

"It's not for sale," Heather said, surprised that this snooping lady would even ask. She didn't sell her paintings. They were a personal, emotional release for her. An expression of her life, her memories, her family, the people in her life, or not. She had painted landscapes, the beach, the sunset, but found the challenge of portraiture much more intriguing. She hated it when her mother's friends or committee members wandered around the estate, pretending to find a bathroom, but were just on a snooping spree.

"Do you need someone to show you where the meeting is?"

"Meeting?"

"For the Winter Ball."

"Oh, that, no, that's all right," Gloria said, glancing at the girl, thinking the blonde looked familiar. So young, so pretty, surely she couldn't be the artist.

"Who's the artist?"

"Does it matter?" Heather leaned forward with cramps. She protectively placed her hand on her stomach while she tried to remember the breathing techniques.

Typical temperamental artist, Gloria thought, smiling. "Do you have any more?" Were there enough paintings to do a show? How she'd love to sponsor one. She loved the law, but she loved discovering new talent even more.

"I . . . oh, my," Heather said, clutching her protruding belly. Contractions had started. Hard ones. She was going to disrupt her mother's meeting, after all.

"Moth-er!"

Chapter Twenty Three

Robbie's phone rang in his New York flat. "Hello?"

"Hey, it's me."

"Heather? What's up?" He hadn't expected to talk to her again so soon.

"I am now the proud mother of a beautiful baby girl."

"A girl?"

"Like the doctor said."

"How is she? How are you?" This is so weird. Seems as if I just talked to you."

"I know. I'm fine. And she is gorgeous."

Robbie knew she would be. "I can't wait to see her, and you."

"When you come out, we'll have the christening."

"I'm ready to be her Godfather." Since he couldn't be her adoptive father. "Tell me about her."

Heather missed Robbie, but now he had his budding career, just like she had with her painting. "She's eight pounds, two ounces, and she has this wonderful, lush, dark head of hair. She's so cute." Just like her father.

"What's her name?"

"Kiki Marie Sanger."

"That's beautiful. So, no more Heather Kane?"

"Nope. Sanger, all the way."

"Where'd you get Kane from anyway?"

"You ever see Citizen Kane?"

Robbie laughed.

"What about the birth certificate?"

"What about it?" Heather knew what he meant, just didn't want to say his name out loud. Writing Lucky's name on the birth certificate had been hard enough, but she did.

"Have you told him yet?"

"No."

He was going to be her second call.

"Are you going to?"

"I plan to, but wanted you to know first." Heather had to change the subject. "How's the play going?"

Fine, if Heather didn't want to talk about Lucky, he wasn't going to push it. "You wouldn't believe it, love. It's a small part, but I actually have lines."

"I'm so proud of you, Robbie." She tried not to laugh, it had only been a few hours since her baby was born, and she still felt raw. Her heart was filled with overwhelming warmth and love, yet her body was sore.

"I have you to thank, sweetie."

"Robbie, you're talented. I always told you so."

"Thanks, but I'm not sure if I could have pulled this off without your encouragement."

"Okay, look, I'll pick you up at the airport."

"Are you kidding? You don't need to do that. Just send your chauffeur." Robbie laughed. He thought it was priceless when Heather told him who she really was. What a family to be a Godfather in. This was okay in his book. "You know, Heather, I can only stay for a day or two, have to get back, but I can stay longer next time."

"How are you and Gabriel managing?"

"I guess we're a bi-coastal couple now."

"Don't make me laugh."

"Love, yuh," Robbie said, then he hung up. He'd wanted to tell her about his night out with the guys, but couldn't remember much about it, except that there was a shot drinking contest with some old guy. Then everything went black.

*   *   *

A white-haired lady in a pink smock came into the hospital room carrying a stack of magazines.

"Thanks, but I don't—"

"Might be your last chance for a while, you're gonna be

busy. But, I would imagine someone like you will have a nanny."

"No, I don't believe in them. I'm going to be taking care of her myself." Heather reached for the phone.

The number was memorized. She started to call there so many times, but couldn't go through with it. What if he'd break her life in two again? Was she strong enough to deal with more heartbreak?

*   *   *

"Come here, bitch," Lucky said. How he got talked into taking care of the cat while J.J. was out of town was beyond him. Why couldn't the cat wait until the maid arrived? Opening the can of tuna-flavored cat food, he coaxed the smelly blob out with a fork, and it plopped into the bowl in a solid mass.

The cat rubbed up against his leg and purred.

"Cat, don't do that."

His cell phone rang, but he ignored it, wiping the cat hair off his chestnut-colored pants.

Heather waited, wondering if he'd answer before she'd hang up.

Bonbon happily ate her food as he tried to rid the fishy smell that caught on his hands.

His phone stopped ringing, so the voice mail kicked in. He'd check his messages later, on the way to the office.

Heather listened as his voice mail came on . . . You have reached Lane Lawson. I'm not available right now, but leave a message at the sound of the beep. His old European dialect seemed so familiar, her heart skipped a beat, but she hung up without leaving a message. What would she say? Surprise—you have a daughter. Oh—and by the way. I'm really a Sanger. If his quest for money drove him away, she wouldn't want it to be the reason it brought him back.

A nurse brought Kiki Marie into the room as Heather set

the phone aside.

"Here you are, Mama," the nurse said, smiling, handed her the baby.

Heather took her infant, unwrapped the blanket, and held her against her bare breast. As the baby suckled, Heather decided she'd call Lucky later.

Chapter Twenty Four

"Kiki Marie Sanger, I baptize thee in the name of the Father, and of the Son, and of the Holy Ghost."

They all smiled, as the ceremony continued. Billy, his wife Patrice, Heather, Robbie, Gabriel and Wanda. Just a small, private ceremony. Performed in the same chapel that Heather had been baptized in.

"That was an exquisite service," Patrice Sanger said, wiping tears from her eyes with a pink silk handkerchief.

Kiki's godmother, Heather's cousin Lola, couldn't be there, so Wanda, her neighbor from Sea Breeze, filled in as her proxy.

"Thank you so much for filling in for Lola," Heather said.

"Don't give it a second thought, dear," Wanda said.

Heather and the others walked out into the garden after the ceremony. A photographer, who'd captured all the important milestones in the Sanger family, waited.

They all took turns holding Kiki for photos. The infant never woke up through the picture taking process, or even during the ceremony, not even when the water was poured on her head. Then all she did was wince.

"I think that's enough pictures," Billy said. He was hungry and wanted to get back to the house, and the huge feast he knew was already prepared.

"She's waking up," Heather said. Watching her daughter crinkle her nose and open her eyes was an event in itself. "I think she's going to smile."

"Darling, she's too young to smile," her mother said.

"Was that really your outfit, Heather?" Gabe interrupted.

"Everybody, ready?" Billy asked, leading the group toward the waiting Rolls-Royce.

"It was a beautiful service." Gabriel gave Heather a hug.

"But I have to get back to the city."

"Don't you want to see the house?" Robbie whispered.

"No, that's okay." He wasn't impressed with the outward displays of wealth like Robbie was.

"I'll meet you at the reception," Wanda said. Excited about seeing the Sanger mansion for the first time, she got in her Honda Accord, ready to caravan to the estate.

Billy opened the door for Patrice first, she would sit in the front, Heather and Robbie were next to each other in the back seat with Kiki in a car seat.

"Nice car," Robbie said, getting into the Rolls Royce. "How much did it—" He felt a jabbing in his ribs.

Heather was glaring at him.

"What?" he whispered. "Just trying to make conversation."

Billy started the car and they headed home. The custom-built car had cost him almost a half a million, but it was worth every penny in entertainment value alone. To see the looks on people's faces when they saw it, especially with an infant car seat in it, was priceless.

"Did you ever tell him?" Robbie's voice was low enough so only Heather would hear.

"I've tried to, but every time I picked up the phone, I hang up. Don't want him to come back for the wrong reason."

"I know, sweetie."

"Robbie, when do you have to go back?"

"You know, New York beckons." His voice became louder when he talked about his passion, the play.

Patrice turned her head. "What are you two whispering about back there?"

"Robbie has to go back to New York." She grinned and pinched Robbie on his knee. "He has a part in Boxcar Mania."

"It's only a small part," Robbie said. He jabbed Heather in the ribs in a playful manner.

Heather gazed at Robbie, "You're coming back for the opening, right?"

"I wouldn't miss that for all the money in Billy Sanger's bank account."

Billy and Patrice glared daggers at him.

"Oh, my Gosh, I'm sorry. I can't believe I just said that." He could feel the blood draining from his face. "Please forgive me, Mr. and Mrs. Sanger."

Patrice didn't know when she and her daughter reconciled, it meant putting up with her friends. Billy didn't know when he and his daughter reconciled, it meant bringing outsiders into the family. Funny, there was always a price in life.

"Don't worry about it," Billy said. "Let's just enjoy the day." But still, he worried.

Chapter Twenty Five

The Opening—San Francisco

Heather glowed in a floor-length, cream-colored, satin halter gown boasting miniature crystal beads that reflected the light and sparkled as much as her radiant blue eyes. The clinging dress showed off her slim figure. She was proud to have reclaimed her girlish shape following the pregnancy. Her long blonde hair was trimmed to a more sophisticated shoulder-length style. She still had her tan, courtesy of a tube. Her little angel and her painting were virtually all she had time for these days.

"Girlfriend, you look positively illegal," Robbie said, from across the room. Heads turned as he brushed by them to reach Heather.

"Robbie, thank you for being here."

"Wouldn't miss it," he said, grabbing a flute of champagne from a passing tray, giving the waiter a wink.

"How's your run going?" she asked, noticing he had a drink, but rationalized that it was okay because it was a special occasion. She glanced around at all the people who had come to the opening. Yet, she was still in disbelief that it all happened so fast. One minute she was a college student, then a mom, and now all this.

"The show is unbelievable. New York is fabulous. So many interesting people. Everybody has a story to tell—"

Gloria interrupted. "How's my beach bunny doing?" She came up behind Heather and squeezed her shoulders.

"Little nervous."

"Don't be, darling, they'll love you." Gloria still could-n't believe her good fortune having stumbled into Heather that day at the Sanger residence.

"Your show is a hit, too, Robbie, from what I hear," Gloria added. "Getting rave reviews."

Robbie blushed. "Thank you." Where'd Gabriel go? He seemed to disappear as soon as they arrived.

"Where is she?" Robbie asked. "Where is my goddaughter?"

"She's over there," Heather said, pointing, "with the nanny."

"Nanny?"

"You know my mother," she said, rubbing her eyebrows. "She hired a baby sitter, but just for tonight. She's from one of those professional services, so she's called a nanny," Heather said, rolling her eyes.

"What's her story?"

"She's a perky girl from France. Daphne's her name. She speaks English, but her accent is as thick as sludge."

Robbie gave a small laugh. Heather always made him feel relaxed. "I'll be back in a jiff." He kissed Heather on her cheek. "I'm gonna go see my godbaby." Robbie disappeared into throngs of chattering voices.

*   *   *

A brand new red Ferrari roared up in front of the gallery. "Perfect, a spot right in front."

"It's a handicap only spot," Abby said, noticing the blue curb.

"When you own a car like this, and I do, you can park anywhere you damn well please."

"A little cranky, are we?" Abby retouched her glossy red lipstick in the vanity mirror. "You're going to have to lighten your mood, or they're going to take that title away from you." She laughed, wondering if there would be photographers and hoping they'd get a good shot of her.

Lucky glared at her. A true beauty of centerfold quality, but he wasn't interested. There was no denying this woman from his office was hot, yet she didn't fill his empty heart.

Ever since that day Heather stormed out on him, his entry into the fast lane had surged like he never expected. The gold dust turned into bars of gold. He'd stayed on at Nomadic, but moved out of J.J.'s condo. Heather never returned any of his phone calls and refused to talk to him. What good did the gold do without someone to share it with?

After a stint in sales, J.J. named him Vice President of Marketing. He was glad his new life afforded him the things he'd always wanted. Like, in addition to the Porsche, a Ferrari. And between his salary, stock options, and the women after him, his life was where he wanted it to be. Almost.

He couldn't get the damn murder out of his head. Like a foggy day, it would always be there, hanging over his head; a memory that would not evaporate no matter how hard he tried to erase it.

As he pulled the sun visor down, a pack of gum slid out, which now replaced his cigarette habit.

"Okay, I'm ready," Abby said, hiding the lipstick tube between her cleavage. She didn't want to be hindered by a purse. A valet opened the car door for her. As she stepped out, she smoothed down her clinging, sizzling-red dress, checking herself in the reflection of the gallery window.

"Who's the huge artist, anyway?" Lucky asked as they walked in.

"Billy Sanger's daughter."

*   *   *

Across the room, Heather was wrapping up her chat with Gloria. "I'll be right back. I'm getting a bit of a headache. And I want to call my parents to see when they're arriving."

"Be quick. Everyone wants to meet you, and I'd like to make a toast," Gloria said. "I've got aspirin if you need it."

"Thanks, I'll be fine, and I won't be long," Heather said. "I'll be in Frederick's office if you need me."

Gloria patted Heather on her butt. "Okay, hurry up, my star."

"Can I get you anything?" a waiter asked Heather as she walked by.

"That's all right, thanks though," she said, glancing back at him. He was smiling at her. He's barking up the wrong tree, Heather thought. She was not interested.

"Okay, baby," he whispered back.

No one could ever compare to Lucky. Would she ever get over him? Did she want to get over him?

Once inside Frederick's office, she turned off the bothersome, overhead fluorescent lighting. Leaving the door slightly open gave her enough light to see but was dim enough to be soothing. The room was quiet, so she savored the time alone before the required mingling.

*   *   *

"Billy Sanger must pay a lot of money to keep his daughter out of the press," Lucky said. He'd never even seen a picture of her.

"I don't think he worries about money." After her sarcastic comment, Abby glanced around for the photographer.

A waiter held a tray in front of her. "Hors d'oeuvre?"

"No thanks," Abby said. She turned to Lucky. "I'll be right back. Why don't you scope out the Sanger princess' artwork? I bet they're just paint by numbers in disguise." Abby laughed as she walked off.

"I don't care about any of these paintings," he said under his breath. He turned to the waiter. "But I will take one of those. Thanks, man." He put the hors d'oeuvre in his mouth and instantly regretted it. "Oh, shit." His throat tightened. He coughed and glanced around for something to drink. He pressed his way through the crowd, ending up at the back of the gallery with a salty taste in his mouth.

He noticed a door that was ajar; he peeked in and saw the outline of a woman in the shadows. She was sitting on top of a desk with her long legs crossed. Her back was toward the door, and she must not have heard him since she hadn't turned to look at him.

"Excuse me. Could you tell me where a thirsty guy can get a drink of plain ol' water?"

The phone fell out of her hand. Her dry throat tightened as if she couldn't swallow or breathe. That breath she'd hoped for had been taken from her. His voice was as smooth as always. Trembling, her often rehearsed speech ran through her mind. Her name was Kiki Marie. She was a Sanger. And, they both wanted - needed - his love. They'd never have to want for anything because they would have each other.

She started to turn, to tell him, but out of the corner of her eyes, something on the desk caught her attention. She glanced down. A magazine she hadn't noticed before stared up at her as if it were trying to send her a secret message. Silicon Sphere magazine, with his photo on the cover. A caption beneath, read, "Bachelor of the Year." In the photo, he was surrounded by beautiful women ogling him, hundred dollar bills coming from his pockets. A lame attempt by the photographer at humor. But, there he was, smiling his million-dollar grin that drew women to him. His charm and self-assured ways moved him through life as though he'd expected things to always go his way.

"You, okay?" he asked. There was something about her.

His voice was as magnetic as ever. She was going to turn around . . . tell him she still loved him . . . feel his arms around her once more . . . tell him he had a daughter in the next room who had his dark hair and her sparkling eyes . . . that their child represented a combination of their souls brought together by love. She was going to tell him that while he may be bachelor of the year, he was also a father.

In the darkness of the room, Lucky thought her silhouette itself was an art form.

"There you are," Abby said, grabbing his arm. "The Sangers are here."

"What? The king and queen themselves?" Lucky asked, laughing.

Heather turned around to watch him walking away, a woman in a firehouse red dress clinging to his side.

*   *   *

"Dear, your parents are here," Gloria said.

Heather bowed her head. She closed her eyes and rubbed them as if it would cure her heartache.

"Heather?"

"Thanks. I'll be right there."

A crowd had gathered around the Sangers and the featured painting of the evening. The centerpiece for the entire exhibit. The one that commanded the most attention. The painting that garnered Gloria's attention that day when she had wandered in by mistake into Heather's art studio. The same painting that everyone wanted to bid on, but weren't allowed to. The only one that wasn't for sale, and that Heather hadn't found the proper title for. For now, the painting was referred to as the Unnamed Portrait.

They all wanted to know about the subject. Who was she? Where did the artist get her inspiration for this piece?

But, Heather would never tell that the idea had come from a memory. The creased and splotchy photograph she had seen at a glance. Yet the viewing was long enough to be remembered forever. Heather would never sell the painting. Someday she planned to give it away to its rightful owner. She'd give it to Lucky so he could have more as a remembrance of his mother than a torn and tattered photograph.

Chapter Twenty Six

Frederick Eaton, art dealer and owner of the Eaton Gallery, stood in front of the highest level of society patrons that had ever been assembled in his place of business. This night belonged to him, and in his mind, would forever entitle him as the reigning king of fine arts of San Francisco. He was a man in charge. And he was at the podium.

"I'd like to thank everyone for coming to the Eaton Gallery this evening." He was quite pleased with the turnout. This new association with the Sanger dynasty would bring his business back on top where it belonged following several months of sluggish sales.

"And, now," he said, "without further delay, please welcome Ms. Gloria Harwood."

As she took the microphone from Frederick, Gloria glanced around the room for Rocco, the freelance photographer she'd hired for the event. She hoped he'd get a good shot of her and that her gold lamé dress would look good on camera. The dress was pricey and was quite a departure from her usual staunch business suits.

"Thank you, Mr. Eaton," Gloria said, nodding, turning to the crowd.

"Good evening, everyone. As many of you know, I am senior law partner at Bender, Baines and Harwood." A little plug didn't hurt. "But that's not why I'm here this evening." Of course, it was. "I'm here to tell you a story. Quite by accident I stumbled upon Miss Heather Sanger not so long ago." Because she'd really meant to stumble into the Billy man that day. "I saw something in her that I don't think she'd known in herself. She has raw talent, only beginning to emerge, with a brilliant future in front of her. These paintings here tonight are just to give you a sampling of the talent this young girl has."

How Gloria loved discovering new talent, it was the only thing that competed with the satisfaction of being an attorney. Plus the publicity she garnered for being involved in the arts hadn't hurt her law practice a bit, not to mention the partnership she now felt existed between herself and the Sangers.

"Miss Sanger is graciously donating all of her proceeds from the sale of her art to the Bay Area Homeless Coalition. So get your checkbooks out, and have fun shopping."

"Of course," Gloria added, "in addition to purchasing Miss Sanger's art, any additional donation you chose to make to the coalition is most appreciated."

"And, expected," Abby said to the stud standing next to her. Interesting combination, she thought, a tuxedo and cowboy boots. Memories of her mother's voice popped into her head . . . posture Abigail . . . posture, you'll never get a man without good posture. She arched her back causing her chest to stick out further than it already was.

Abby watched him out of the corner of her eye. She was waiting for the moment when she caught him in the act of peeking at her cleavage.

Bingo, she thought. She hadn't worn a low-cut, red-hot dress for nothing. She'd come with Lucky, but would go home with someone else. Someone with even more greenbacks. Someone she might even convince to take a quick trip to Vegas. Maybe even get married. Abby believed in utilizing her talents to the fullest, never wasting an opportunity when one was presented.

"In a few moments, Miss Sanger will tell you all about this very worthy cause."

"A very worthy cause," Sasha Dunn whispered to John.

John Dunn was standing next to his wife Sasha and on the opposite side, a dark-haired model-type with unbelievable tits, who appeared lonely.

"Indeed," John said to his wife, but looking at the woman in the red dress. Her cleavage seemed to be taunting

him, and he swallowed hard, then felt a jabbing in his ribs
coming from Sasha, who knew just what he was thinking after
years of experience.

Sasha leaned over to the bimbo. "He's married, honey.
Move on."

Abby was disappointed, this one looked so her type,
oozing sex appeal and money. She could tell that just by looking at him. The married part didn't bother her if he didn't
care. She figured there were lots of other wealthy, unmarried
men in this room tonight. With any luck, she'd find one who
didn't have to contend with a divorce first. Losing half their
money in a settlement before she got her hooks into them
wouldn't be part of the equation.

As John watched the long-legged sex siren walk away, his
eyes were glued to the outline of her firm buttocks through
her skintight dress. "Jesus," he said, under his breath.

"Put your eyeballs back in their sockets, mister," Sasha
said, followed by a smile to her husband.

John grinned. He was glad his wife enjoyed sex, and he
didn't have to go looking for it, but if he did, it wouldn't be
hard to find. Now his thoughts turned from sex, which he'd
get later from his horny wife, to money.

The term "worthy cause" that Gloria had used, stuck in
his head like an overdue library book. Most causes were
worthy, was this one any different? There were so many
needs in the community, a never-ending event it seemed.
But, he surmised, the bottom line was that he was honored
to be invited to these events, even if it were because of his
bank balance. As much as he felt uncomfortable at these
affairs, he usually ended up having a good time. He'd get his
checkbook out, figuratively speaking. Did anyone even carry
a checkbook anymore? Tonight, he'd buy a few paintings
and make the expected contribution. His wife would be
happy, but also, deep inside, it would please him. He
noticed the woman in the red dress had sauntered up to
another unsuspecting sucker.

Gloria nodded to the headwaiter at the back of the room.

As if on cue, waiters appeared with trays of fluted glasses filled with Dom Perignon.

"If you don't already have a glass, please take some bubbly," Gloria said. She waited until the crowd settled down. Raising her glass, the audience followed suit. "Here's to you, Heather Sanger. Your talent rides on the stars."

"Here, here!" the crowd said in unison, cheering and filled with true glee.

Heather's parents beamed with pride.

Walking up to center stage, Heather shook hands with Frederick and Gloria, then took the spotlight.

"I guess it's my turn to say a few words." How she hated speaking in public. "First, on behalf of the recipients from tonight's event, I'd like to thank you from the bottom of my heart."

Everyone applauded.

"Also, I'd like to extend a very special thank you to Gloria, who convinced me to share my art with others." This wasn't as bad as she'd expected.

"Now to my parents, Billy and Patrice Sanger. There were times when we didn't always see eye to eye, but we used our love to guide us." Heather smiled at her parents. "I love you both," she said, blowing them a kiss.

The cheers grew in volume.

Billy and Patrice waved to everyone, and together nodded their approval. Patrice mouthed I love you to Heather, and Billy gave her the thumbs up.

Billy knew he'd get grief over what was coming next, but he didn't care. He was ready for whatever was lobbed his way from the shocking announcement that was about to bounce from the walls, reverberating into the universe.

"Now, I'd like to give you all a wake up call," Heather said. "Look to the left of you, then to the right."

Everyone glanced around, curious.

"We are the fortunate ones, the ones who will never experience homelessness in our lives . . . but not necessarily. Circumstances sometimes spin out of our control for people of all walks of life. When you think homeless, you may envision drug addicts or drunks on the street begging for whiskey, money, or their next fix. In most cases, homelessness is temporary for many decent people.

"Tonight, there will be an untold number of men, women and yes, children, spending the night out there without a roof over their heads.

"The Bay Area Homeless Coalition is working toward changing that. How you might ask? For example, one component that the coalition, in cooperation with the local government, is working on is to convert existing, vacant buildings into a safe haven. A place for the temporarily displaced to call home. A place where people in need of housing cannot only use the facilities to feed their bellies, but their souls, as well." Just like she'd done with Lucky.

"As I was saying, homeless people come in all shapes and sizes. I asked you a few minutes ago to look to your left and your right, but now I ask you to look at me. Yes, look at me. I was once homeless."

An audible gasp passed through the stunned audience. All eyes turned from Heather to her parents, Mr. and Mrs. Billy Sanger, richest couple in the Bay Area, the country, if not the world.

"It's okay," Billy said to those around him offering their condolences over the mortification and shock they wrongly assumed he must've been feeling.

Heather gave a small smile. "I don't think I need to explain all the details, except to say, anyone can end up on the street at some point in their lives. Regardless of their own personal circumstances. Our place is not to judge, rather it is our duty to help."

Billy, Patrice and Heather had discussed her courageous speech ahead of time, and their conclusion was that they had no secrets. Not anymore. If telling the truth helped others, Heather was free to discuss what she'd been through, what they'd been through, in any capacity.

His daughter had run away from home as a rebellious teenager and lived on the streets for a time, but the family had made amends through counseling and hard work. They'd benefited from the sessions, bettering their relationship. Billy figured that the love they felt and the understanding they gained was something people wouldn't begin to understand.

"If anyone would like to talk to me about this further," Heather said, "I'll be available for your questions.

"In addition, as Gloria said earlier, any purchase you make of my art, tonight or in the future, will directly impact the Bay Area Homeless Coalition. Volunteers are here, representing the coalition, so please see them about your pledges. In gratitude for your own blessings, dig deep. Please be generous."

As Heather waited for the thunderous applause to subside, she turned to a nearby waiter. "Can you please get me something to drink?"

Wiping a tear that had fallen down her cheek, she took a deep breath as she tried to compose herself. She'd gotten through what she considered the business part of her speech, and now it was time to get personal. Knowing Lucky would find out this way was a risk, but one she was willing to take.

Lucky was about to figure out that he had a daughter. Should've told him in private. But she couldn't stop now. This news she'd been planning for him had meant so much. She didn't want him to find out this way, but it was too late for that now.

"Thank you," she said, as the waiter returned with a glass. Heather took a sip of champagne, moistening her dry throat.

Glancing around the room, Heather wondered where Lucky was standing. Images seemed to blur, and all the people who were staring back at her seemed to meld together into one unit, a finished jigsaw puzzle that she felt was about to break apart. What would he say? How would he react? Though Kiki was only an infant, would Lucky recognize his own flesh and blood? She felt a nudging on her arm.

Turning to Gloria, Heather noticed a concerned look on her face.

"Heather, you okay?" The poor girl looked stricken.

"I'm fine." Only she wasn't fine. She'd had to get through the rest of her speech. Through the inevitable.

"Don't be nervous. You're doing great, and you certainly have their attention now, kiddo," she said, rubbing Heather's back between her shoulder blades.

"I ... I ..." Heather had instructed Daphne to bring Kiki up to the main gallery when she called her, but now she wondered if that had been a mistake. To present her daughter to the child's father in public like this seemed almost the sacrificial lamb ritual. What was she thinking?

Though Kiki wouldn't remember the day, Heather would tell her all about it when she was old enough. The day her mommy debuted not only as an artist, but also as a community advocate.

Remorse filled Heather's heart for not telling Lucky the day she'd discovered she was pregnant. Should've told him the day Kiki was born, or perhaps when she was baptized. The more time that went by, the harder telling him had become.

Heather wondered if anyone would mind if she slipped her shoes off. They'd been an uncomfortable choice, but she decided bare feet would be rude with this black-tie convention.

"I'd like to thank the person who has taught me about life. The person who has inspired me the most." Thinking about how much her daughter had changed her life, Heather smiled. Remorse was replaced with pride. She was going to be fine.

"Although, she's too young to understand all this, I'd like to thank my baby girl, Kiki Marie Sanger, the most well-behaved child in the world, for allowing me time to be an artist." There, she'd said it. Now he would know the truth. Lucky would know her true station in life . . . the mother of his child. He'd know she'd given birth to his child, wouldn't he?

"Daphne, could you bring Kiki forward now?"

An eternity seemed to pass when in reality it had only been mere seconds. Would Lucky say anything, or come up on stage to meet his daughter?

The French nanny was taking her sweet time. "I suppose this is a sign that my daughter will always keep me waiting." She laughed, and the crowd followed suit, easing the tension.

Gloria leaned toward Heather. "Never mind, dear, it's a nice gesture, but unnecessary."

"I guess she must be napping," Heather said to the crowd.

Everyone laughed, but there was an undercurrent of nervousness throughout.

"In conclusion, thank you for coming. Have a wonderful evening." Tossing the microphone to Gloria, she hurried away from the podium.

Everyone clapped politely, and the most gossipy of the socialites turned to the nearest person to chat about Heather's revealing speech.

Heather dashed to the back of the gallery, figuring the nanny took her into the office to change her or to let her sleep, but she wanted to check on her just the same.

Entering the room, Heather was startled to find that they weren't there. Kiki's diaper bag was on the floor next to the portable bassinet they'd brought, but it was empty, except for Kiki's blanket.

Heather hurried back to the main room, but now everything seemed different, as if she were having an out-of-body experience. Surveying the room, she could see mouths moving, but no sound seemed to be coming from them, it was as if she were watching TV on mute. Turning to her mother, she hoped that she would wake her from this nightmare.

"You look like you've seen a ghost," Patrice said.

"Mother, Kiki wasn't back there." Heather's voice sounded confused and terror-filled. "I thought maybe Daphne was changing her in the bathroom. Knocking on the door brought no reply."

"Well, where is she then?" Patrice thought her daughter was in serious need of a makeup retouch and wondered if she had rouge in her purse.

"Mom, I don't know where Kiki is, and I don't see the damn nanny, either."

"Maybe your father, Robert or that Gabe fellow has her."

"You know something weird, Mom? I don't see Robbie or Gabriel either."

Patrice began to perspire under her Donatello Versace gown. "Now, now, dear, I'm sure the baby's fine, don't fret about her. That's what I hired a nanny for, so you wouldn't have to worry yourself about the baby. Instead, I wanted you to enjoy your party and have some fun for a change."

She knew Heather had felt uncomfortable about leaving her baby for the evening and thought that having the nanny at the event was the perfect solution, but now her mother's intuition rang out loud and clear that she'd made an egregious error.

Brianna Montgomery had suggested the nanny agency. Ask for Daphne, she'd told Patrice. When Brianna's daughter and her husband went on an impromptu African safari, they'd left their five-month-old daughter with Brianna and her husband, Randall. After one morning of baby-sitting, Brianna found Daphne through a nanny agency that her next-door neighbor recommended. For three weeks, Daphne watched the baby, and Brianna didn't miss one committee meeting.

A heaviness pressed on Patrice's chest as her worst fears of a kidnapping were coming to the forefront of her scrambled thoughts.

Heather's heart was going into overtime and felt like it would pound out of her body. Her eyes filled with tears, her body ached with fear. "I never should've brought her. That was stupid planning. I could've left her with Wanda. She would've been safe there."

A few minutes ago, Heather's life seemed perfect, and now it was on the verge of shattering. With desperation, Heather approached Frederick. "Are there any other rooms in this place?"

"Besides the main gallery, there are the office, the store room and the restroom. This studio isn't that big." He had hoped he'd be moving into larger quarters, but if there was a problem here, moving up in the world would be questionable at best.

"Right now, this place feels suffocating."

"The storeroom is in here," Frederick said, pointing.

The room was filled with art pieces, some wrapped in brown paper, others propped on easels, but there was a desolate feel to it. No baby Kiki. No nanny. No Lucky. No Robbie or Gabriel.

Then, Heather noticed a door. "Where does that lead?"

"To the alley where I get my deliveries, but I always keep the door locked," Frederick said, jiggling the door handle to prove his point. "See." The door opened. "That's odd."

"It's more than odd."

Heather pushed past him and rushed outside. The dark alley was deserted, except for a cat sitting in the middle of the street. A light over the exit door of the gallery was flickering, and looked as if it would burn out any minute. Heather noticed a garbage bin alongside the back of the building. She ran to it and tried to lift the lid, but it was too heavy.

Frederick dashed over and helped her.

The vile stench coming from inside the bin made Heather want to retch. "Oh, God," she said. "Smells like rotting fish."

"Probably is," he said. "There's a cafe over there. It's

closed now, but the smell is probably from discarded food."

"Let's go back inside," Heather said. "There's nothing here."

When they dropped the lid, it made a loud crashing sound, which scared the cat that disappeared down the alley.

Back inside the storeroom, Heather was frightened and frustrated. "I don't believe this," she said, kicking over an easel.

"Did you look in the restroom?" Frederick asked, leaning over and retrieving the easel from the floor. Setting it back up, he noticed that one of the legs would need repairing.

"Of course, I did," Heather said, "but I'll check again."

She knocked on the restroom door. "Hello? Is there anyone in there?"

"Bathroom's taken," a male voice shouted back, clearly annoyed at the intrusion.

"Is Kiki in there?"

"Ahh . . . no, she isn't."

Listening, she could hear muffled voices. She turned the doorknob, but it was locked. The voice sounded like a man speaking, but more like a murmur, and it sounded familiar. She tried to make out the words.

"You are so beautiful, ba . . . by."

Heather slapped hard on the door with her hands, which were becoming redder with each slap. "Open this door right now, you son-of-a-bitch."

Billy, who'd been told by Patrice what was going on, joined Heather. "Let me handle this," he said, shoving her aside. He took one step back, then with one fierce ram of his shoulder, the door broke open.

A waiter ran out. His shirt unbuttoned, his hairy chest exposed. "What the hell did you do that for?"

Daphne ran out after him. "What eeze it? An earthquake?"

"Where is she?" Heather demanded.

"Who?" Daphne asked, straightening her skirt.

"Who?" Heather asked in disbelief. She had moved into an arena of frenzied emotions that were about to render her incapable of controlling her actions.

Daphne waved her arms in the air, trying to explain in broken English. "I left her in thee office," she said, sounding more like a question than a statement. "But only for a moment. Thee babee was sleeping."

This irresponsible Parisian bitch was pissing Heather off. Did this woman not give a shit about her charge? "Well, she's not fine now. My baby is missing."

"Well, I didn't take thee babee. I just thee nanny."

"That's right, and you're supposed to be watching her." This was the nanny from hell, of that Heather was convinced.

"Yes, madam, but you're thee mere, how you say, mother? And you don't know where thee babee is?"

"You goddamn bitch." Heather said, lunging toward Daphne, grabbing her long black hair in the process. The nanny from hell was about to get her perky eyes gouged out.

Daphne fought back, her long fingernails to Heather's face, drawing blood. She gave a kick to Heather's stomach. She knew her days of being an American nanny were over, so what did she care if the rich bitch got hurt?

Billy stepped in and intervened. As he pulled the two women apart, this was not the way he imagined the night would have turned out.

"I'll be back out in the gallery," Heather said, storming off.

Heather glanced around, and at the sudden realization of the magnitude the horrible turn of events had brought, she felt as if a tornado had just ripped through her digestive track. Clutching her stomach, she ran back into the bathroom.

The nanny and the waiter had gone their separate ways. Heather didn't care if they dropped off the face of the earth or if she ever saw them again, whichever came first.

Dropping to the cold, hard, linoleum floor, her fingers gripped the rim of the toilet bowl. She threw up the champagne from earlier. Begging for mercy, she silently bargained with God that for any sin she'd committed here on earth, she'd gladly go to hell at the end of her days in exchange for the return of her precious infant.

Her stomach aching, Heather could empty no more. Staggering to the door, she glanced at herself in the mirror. Her strained face was an image that would forever be etched into her memory.

Then, she heard a scream, a horrifying sound that would be forever be burned into her soul.

*   *   *

Patrice had been the first to see it.

"What is it?" Heather asked, dashing from the bathroom.

A crowd had gathered around one of the exhibit pieces. The one that Heather had refused to sell, the one that Heather had painted with love and care, with Lucky in mind. The one that she'd give him, someday.

"Heather, look," her mother said, nodding at the painting.

A note scrawled on a cocktail napkin stuck to the painting said it all. "Look No Further—We Got the Sanger Heir."

"Did anybody see who did this?" Billy asked, his voice filled with rage as he pushed his way through the crowd.

Those closest to Patrice when she screamed were aware of the note, others farther away had no idea what was going on, other than a commotion of some sort on one side of the gallery.

Abby wondered if all the high-society parties turned out like this. Maybe, this was interactive theater. She couldn't wait to tell Lane . . . Lucky Star, what he'd missed. Where had he disappeared to anyway?

"Call the police," a male voice cried out.

Heather removed the note from the painting, and thin,

fine strands of chewed gum followed. She felt the blood drain from her head. "Oh, my God," she said, her hands trembling. Her voice was almost inaudible. "Oh, my God, I don't believe it."

"Take care of her, Patrice," Billy said, noticing that Heather appeared ashen, perhaps ready to faint. Billy rushed to the podium. Grabbing the microphone, he made an announcement. "Can I have everyone's attention please? Something terrible has happened. My granddaughter is missing, and we need your help. Someone must've seen or heard something."

Wiping his forehead with a cotton handkerchief embroidered with his initials, Frederick sweated. This disaster would ruin him.

Gloria, standing next to Patrice and Heather, knew that anything she'd say to Heather at this point would only upset her more. There was no soothing a near hysterical woman, but she'd give it a try.

"Dear, I've lived in San Francisco a very long time, and this big city is just one small town. We'll find her. We'll find the person or persons behind this horrendous crime. They'll pay for this."

Crime? Pay for it? How had things spun out of control so fast?

Glancing around the room, Heather wished everyone would leave, but knew they couldn't. They shouldn't. She kept telling herself over and over again, she had to stay in control, and she'd already lost it once. Staying calm was impossible, but she had to try, she had to stop freaking out. Were the cops ever going to get here?

"Don't anybody leave this building," Billy said at the top of his lungs. Then, he noticed a photographer taking pictures. He dropped the microphone and approached him.

Rocco had been working like mad, snapping photos, until he stopped to make a call.

"Did your camera catch anything?"

"Just the reactions of the faces, but that's not what you meant, I presume."

"Wise ass, huh? By the way, I don't want any of the pictures you took in here to show up on Drudge, or anywhere else for that matter."

Yeah, right, Rocco thought. He was already making deals to the highest bidder.

*   *   *

Officer Dan Rodriguez and his partner Matt Brady had been patrolling the neighborhood in the west side of the city when the call came in. They parked their squad car in front of the gallery and rushed inside.

"I'm Officer Rodriguez, this is my partner, Officer Brady. We got a call. Something about a missing kid."

Officer Rodriguez had been on the force for ten years, never tiring of it. The electricity of the city was his lifeblood, providing him adrenaline nutrition to get through the day. Each call was like a snack, fueling him with energy and sustenance.

"She's not a kid, only an infant," Heather corrected. "Here, look." She thrust the note at the officer's face. "My baby's been kidnapped!"

"How many people have touched this?" Of course, the note and other evidence would be a matter for forensics, but he figured he'd ask.

"I don't know," Heather said, wiping her nose with a lace hanky.

"About the note?"

"We've all touched it—okay? You happy now?"

Heather's mother put her arm around her. "It'll be okay, dear." But, inside, Patrice worried. She and Billy use to worry about this exact thing when Heather was a child. Kidnapping was always a fear with a family of their stature. That was why they hadn't wanted her to go off and live on her own, the fear was every bit as real as the sun rising in the East.

"If we could have everyone move into this room," Officer Brady said, waving his arms as if he were directing traffic.

Officer Rodriguez glanced around the room full of classy folks who seemed to be eavesdropping on every word exchanged between him and the distraught woman.

"Is there somewhere private we can talk?" he asked.

"Use my office," Frederick offered.

Billy, Patrice, Heather and Officer Rodriguez went into Frederick's office while the other officer searched the premises.

The detective's eyes narrowed as he spoke. "Let's go over the obvious. What about the spouse? The child's father? Is there a custodial dispute?"

"Heather's not married," Billy said, his voice angered. "Shouldn't we call the FBI?"

The officer pressed on. "A disgruntled ex or a jilted boyfriend perhaps?"

This guy was annoying the hell of out Billy. "Do you know who I am?"

"Yes, sir, I do. And don't worry about the FBI, if this is, indeed, determined to be a kidnapping, they're never far behind." But if he solved this case first, he'd be the hero.

"There's no disgruntled spouse, ex or otherwise," Billy said.

"Lucky was here tonight," Heather said, her voice but a whisper.

"Lucky?" Officer Rodriguez asked.

"He's the father of my baby."

Heather looked into the officer's dark eyes, and thought they looked kind. She shook her head. "Lucky never would have done this." But, in the back of her mind, she thought about the gum on the back of the note, but that didn't mean anything. "He didn't even know Kiki Marie existed before tonight." No, he never would've done this.

"Let me get this straight, the father of the missing child was here tonight, discovered for the first time that the infant was his, and now they've both disappeared into thin air?"

"I'm gonna kill him," Billy said over the realization and horror that it appeared Lucky had stolen Kiki.

Anger turned to guilt when Billy knew he should've protected his family better with tighter security. He should've had his team there at the event. That had been a horrendous lapse of judgment caused by a lack of forethought. The baby was supposed to be at home with the staff, behind the stronghold of their estate.

Not being told of the last minute change of plans made Billy feel out of control, and now helpless. But his level head told him that there was nothing he could do about that now. The thing he was certain of was that he would find his granddaughter if it killed him, or whoever inadvertently got in the way, Lucky included.

Chapter Twenty Seven

The kidnappers congratulated themselves for pulling off the caper of the century. Driving through the streets of the city, they planned on hanging out for a while before making their next move.

"Good idea, to use the party for the snatch."

"And to think, we were just going to use it as a social engagement. A chance to strategize, to go over our options. To begin to blend in with these people, then we'd hit them when they least expected it."

"I couldn't believe the lack of security. Then, when I heard the baby was there, I couldn't believe our luck. It was the opportunity that we'd been waiting for. Too good to pass up. I thought we were going to have a stakeout for weeks, but this way was so easy. The kid was just handed to us on a silver platter."

"After I called you, you got to the back alley, quick."

"Always gotta be ready. Timing is everything."

"Should we call the family yet?"

"No way, let them sweat it out. I got us a room at a flea bag motel, we'll hole up there for a while."

"Yeah, I'm starving, anyway, something I ate made me sick. I gotta eat something else."

"We'll get some food, besides I bet you can't wait to hold the baby."

"Hell, no."

"Really? I'm surprised. Thought that kind of thing was instinct."

"Maybe it is with some people, but not with me."

The abducted infant was awake, trembling on the back floor of the car, where they'd put her when they sped away.

As they drove through the city, the pair shook their heads at the ease of it all.

"The waiter was bought off for next to nothing. Only had to slip him a C-note."

"What an idiot, he probably would've hit on nanny for nothing."

"Didn't take much to get her away from the kid, though, did it? Whetting her sexual appetite with that waiter was a snap."

The pair continued to relive the past few minutes, congratulating themselves. The paid-off waiter distracted the nanny quite well. In an instant, the baby was snatched and off to the getaway car that waited in the dark alley. Engine running and all set to flee.

Kiki was scared, cold and hungry. Listening for the sound of familiar voices that normally comforted her, she heard none. Waiting for the arms that normally held her, she felt none. Her breathing grew rapid.

"That kid's awful quiet back there."

"Count your blessings."

At first, her cries were whimpers. Then she grew louder with each gasp of air, until becoming a high-pitched wail, shattering the nerves of the kidnappers.

"What's kid's problem?" the driver asked.

"How should I know?"

"Shut it up. But remember, we want a quiet baby, not a dead one."

Chapter Twenty Eight

"Robbie, where the hell have you been all night? I've been calling you for hours."

"Right here at home. Geeze, Heather, I'm sorry for slipping out of the party early, but you know, Gabe and I never get a chance to see each other anymore, and we—"

Heather interrupted him. "Kiki's been kidnapped."

"That's not funny. Don't even joke about that."

"Someone took her from the gallery. They left a note. My baby." Heather couldn't hold back any longer. She couldn't be strong, anymore. But she was afraid if she started to cry, she'd never be able to stop.

"I don't believe it—can't be," Robbie said.

"It's true," she said, her voice cracking.

"Take a deep breath, and tell me what happened."

"I don't know what happened. She was there one minute and gone the next. Now, we're back home. We stayed at the gallery until almost dawn, then decided to come back to my parents' place, even though I would've rather gone to my house. None of that matters now. The FBI has all the phones tapped. I'm calling from a cell." She felt she couldn't breathe. She needed Kiki Marie.

"I'll be there as soon as I can."

Then, Heather heard Robbie in the background. "Gabriel, you're not going to believe this." He hung up.

Downstairs, the twenty-foot dining room table had been set up as a command post. She could hear the muffled sound of voices and phones ringing and beeping. If only she could hear her baby's cry. Deep within, she, in her heart of hearts, knew her baby was crying out for her mommy. Heather pulled a teddy bear out of the vacant crib. She clutched it against her chest and her pounding heart.

She'd changed out of her dress from the night before

and was wearing her mother's robe. Maybe wearing it
would bring her maternal comfort. If only she could give
maternal comfort to her own daughter. Feeling into the
deep pockets of the robe, she found a pacifier. But there
was something else. A bottle of her mother's tranquilizers.
She opened the bottle.

With a handful of pills in the palm of her hand, Heather
took a quick look around the room for something to swallow
them with.

Chapter Twenty Nine

Lucky had left the party feeling depressed and alone. What a wasted evening all the way around. Abby dumped him. He hadn't had the pleasure of meeting Billy Sanger or his mysterious, well-hidden secret of a daughter—the artist. And he couldn't get that damn caviar taste out of his mouth. Why would anyone think raw fish eggs make the perfect touch to any appetite tray?

After changing out of his tux and into his comfortable sweats, he grabbed a beer and sat down on the sofa to watch the news. Not moving from the sofa, he soon fell asleep.

Bonbon, J.J.'s cat, was asleep on his chest. He'd made up with the feisty feline, after a rough start, and now the furry bundle stayed with him while J.J. was out of town. When was she coming back, anyway? She said it would be a short trip, but she was gone longer than her usual business sojourns.

Sometime during the night, something startled both of them. Bonbon jumped off, her claws digging into his flesh. Half asleep, Lucky got up and turned the TV off. Someone was at the front door, and they weren't quiet about it. With his head leaning close to the door, he was now fully awake.

"I've got a gun," Lucky lied. Then, the door opened with force, cracking his nose.

Three masked men entered the house. Two of the would-be burglars tackled him to the ground, while the third ran through the house, screaming. "Where is she?"

"Who?" Lucky uttered in disbelief. Then, a set of fierce hands wrapped around his neck, cutting off his circulation.

"You're gonna kill him, asshole. He's no good to us dead," one of the men said.

Lucky was released from the strangulation hold, only to be beaten. Two against one, the odds were not in his favor. Pushed down to the floor, the heavier of the two sat on his chest, compressing all his air from his lungs, until his body went limp. Then, just when he thought he was a dead man, the guy released him. Blood dripped down his face and seeped into his mouth, causing him to swallow blood. When he tried to stand, he couldn't. This was a horrible nightmare. A real one, not the ones that chased him in his sleep. Kneeling on the floor, his throbbing head hung in confusion.

"She's not here," the third one said, after ransacking through the house.

"Whatever you want. You got the wrong guy," Lucky said, spitting out blood.

"You Lucky Lukovich?"

His past had finally caught up with him. His ship was sunk. All that he had obtained would be gone. He'd be back where he started. With nothing but the clothes on his back, and a dream in his heart.

"What do you want me to say?"

"Like we said, where's the baby?"

"You mean, J.J.?"

"This guy's got no brains. The baby. Your daughter."

Lucky wiped the oozing blood away from his nose. "Okay, now I know you got the wrong person. I don't have a daughter. Don't have any kids."

"We mean Heather's baby?"

"Heather? As in Kane?"

"He's got a brain, after all."

"That's right, Heather Kane."

The security team was the best in the private business. They were paid to know everything. They worked exclusively for the big guy, and they'd watched Heather grow up, even kept an eye on her in Sea Breeze, where she'd lived as Heather Kane. They'd parked on the street where she lived. They protected her without her knowing, and this guy they never liked.

They just should've been there tonight. Bad call not to be. If they didn't find who stole the baby, it would be not only their jobs, but also their heads on the cutting block.

"I don't believe what you're saying about a kid," Lucky said.

"Believe it—you're a daddy."

"Come on, let's go," the apparent leader of the trio said, pulling his woolen mask off. "He's clean."

As the men headed toward the front door, one of them turned around. "Oh, and by the way, your kid's been kidnapped, and if you don't produce her, you're a dead man." He might've been clean, but he was still a suspect.

His head raking in confusion, Lucky was clear of one thing. The time had come. God had punished him for his sins, sins that he'd inherited through the bloodline. Dizzy and light-headed, he tried to reach for the phone, but it was a futile effort. Stumbling onto the sofa, he collapsed. Words echoed through his mind before blacking out, daughter . . . kidnapped . . . dead man.

Chapter Thirty

Heather stayed secluded in the baby's upstairs nursery. Before Kiki was born, her mother had it decorated in white with faint yellow accents. Right now, Heather was using the room as a sanctuary. With all sorts of thoughts swimming through her head, she prayed. "Dear God, I know you think I didn't want her . . . at first. Please forgive me. I'll do anything. Take me, but not my baby." Then she collapsed onto the floor. Her life was over.

Winslow poked his head on the door, opening it with his broad nose. He walked over to her, and licked her face.

"Go away," she said, as she pushed his solid body away.

The dog wouldn't give up. He walked around her twice, then beside her.

She put the pacifier that she'd been holding onto in her pocket and removed the bandanna from around the dog's neck. As she used it to wipe the beads of perspiration from her face, the dog watched with droopy eyes.

"I know," she said. Had he been reading her mind? "I've been calling Lucky all night, too. There's no answer, but Daddy said he sent someone to find him. Besides, he never would've done this."

The dog put his nose in the air and cried out in a short, sharp howl.

Reaching for the cell phone, she started to dial Lucky's number.

Before Heather got an answer, she heard steps down the hall coming toward the room.

"Heather?" Her father's voice.

She jumped. "Yes?" She hit the cancel button on the phone.

Looking up, she was amazed at how calm he appeared. Standing in the doorway with his arm resting on the door jam, he was wearing faded jeans and a T-shirt that read, "Bridge School Benefit" on it. She thought he looked so young, yet he was so wise.

Heather took a deep breath. Her chest hurt, and she wondered if she were having a heart attack. Maybe, she should've taken the pills earlier, but her second thoughts had given her enough time to realize it would've been a mistake.

The silence in the air was deafening. Heather was afraid of the news her father must be bringing.

"She's okay," he said.

"Thank God." She could breathe again. Air entered her lungs, seemingly for the first time in hours.

Billy squinted and rubbed his eyes. They'd been told Kiki was alive and well, but he couldn't accept that his worst fears had finally transpired. A kidnaping.

"Daddy, who are they?"

"I don't know. But, we now know what they want. They've just called their demands in."

"What do they want?"

"Ten million."

"Oh, Daddy, I'm sorry."

"Don't be ridiculous. You don't have to be sorry, this isn't your fault. You know I don't care about the money."

"Who would do such a thing? Who would want to hurt my baby? You know it couldn't have been Lucky."

"I don't know, sweetheart." The jury was still out on Lucky as far as Billy Sanger was concerned.

"I should've better protected you, Heather, you and Kiki." His eyes filled with moisture.

"Now, who's being ridiculous, Daddy. There's only so much a person can do. I've told you how I feel. If I can't live my life free, then what kind of a life is that? Once freedoms are lost, life becomes a prison."

"I'm going downstairs," he said. Having a philosophical discussion was something they could do later, not now.

"When will we get her back?" she asked before he left.

"They want the money sent to an offshore account. We're working on it. The FBI is on top of everything. This will be over soon, and you'll have your baby girl back. We'll all have her back. Then we can talk."

Billy went back downstairs. The Sangers' normally quiet, serene estate had been turned into a movie set. But, this was real, not a Hollywood back lot.

*   *   *

"Hello?" Lucky could barely move. If his body hadn't hurt so much, he would've sworn that he was dead and waking up in hell.

"Lucky?"

"Yeah?"

"It's me."

"Heather?"

"Yeah."

"What the hell is going on? These guys were here, beat the shit out of me."

"I'm sorry."

"Is it true?"

"Our baby girl—she's been kidnapped."

"I don't believe it. Why didn't you tell me about her? You didn't even tell me you were pregnant. Heather, why? Why didn't you tell me?" He was so angry with her right now, but much angrier with himself for becoming so upset.

Feeling like his father, Lucky knew he had to fight off the intrusion inside his head that his father had planted there long ago. Hatred.

Heather stood near the window. The vast grounds that she looked out onto, never felt so small, so much like a prison. "I'm sorry . . . I—"

"Why in the world would anybody want to kidnap her?"

"I can explain that—"

"Whatever the kidnapper wants, I'll pay it. Money is no

object." For Heather and the daughter he'd just discovered was his, he'd pay the moon. If he didn't have enough money, he'd find it, somehow.

"They want ten million."

"What?"

"It's okay, my—" A commotion that permeated all the way to the second floor stopped her.

"Heather, hurry!"

Winslow was barking and running around in circles as if he understood the English language.

Heather's mother ran upstairs screaming. "We heard from them. A deal's been made. Let's go get her!"

"Lucky, it's okay, now. I'll call you back as soon as I can." After she hung up, she knelt down and thanked God.

Lucky felt relief, happiness and despair all at the same time.

Downstairs, Billy explained to Heather that the call they'd been waiting for had come in. Once the ten million was confirmed transferred, the baby would be left on the eastern pedestrian pathway located at the base of the southeast Tower One on the Golden Gate Bridge.

Heather, her father, mother, several officers, and FBI agents scrambled for their respective cars.

"Let's move it," an FBI agent said.

Chapter Thirty One

A fleet of vehicles caravanned north up the freeway.

"I thought I said, no media," Billy said, looking out the car window at a helicopter overhead.

"It's one of ours," the agent said.

"Listen to the man," Patrice said, patting Billy on his shoulder. She sat in the back seat of the agent's car, and Heather was next to her.

"I don't want this turning into a media circus," Billy said.

The agent who was driving turned to look at Billy for a second, still in disbelief that he was riding in a car with the great Billy Sanger. But being in the business as long as he had been, he became somewhat immune to celebrity. "Mr. Sanger, my priority is getting your grandchild back. But, in an abduction, the media can help." He stepped on the gas pedal a bit harder. If he didn't get her back, he feared his head would roll like a bowling ball. God only knew what kind of power this man yielded.

The sirens would be turned off when they approached the bridge for fear of scaring the kidnappers more than they already planned to.

Heather was talking into a cell phone, her voice a whisper. "Lucky, meet us at the bridge."

"Which one?"

"The Golden Gate. South entrance."

"Is that where she'll be?"

"Supposedly. And, Lucky?"

"Yeah?"

"I'll explain everything there." The line went dead.

*   *   *

As the bridge entered into view, Heather noticed that the fog was so dense it seemed to hug the orange towers pointing toward heaven. The daily morning commuter traffic over the bridge had subsided. The flow seemed smooth, running at a steady pace. The usual pedestrians, bicyclists and tourists crossed the bridge on the sidewalks that ran parallel to the traffic lanes in each direction. The heavy fog held no one back.

Nearing the entrance to the bridge, the caravan broke up into smaller units before reaching the toll booths. Some of the cars disappeared from view, and Heather wondered where they were going. Don't worry about it, she was told. Yeah, right.

The car that the Sangers were in abruptly veered off the road, just before the toll booths. They drove down a steep and winding driveway, ending up at Fort Point.

The historic brick fortress was built to prevent hostile enemies from entering San Francisco Bay. On one side, the vast Pacific Ocean, on the other side, the bay. Today the hostile enemy was unknown, yet a battle was being prepared to be fought.

"Stay in the car," one of the agents said as he got out of his own vehicle in a hurry.

"I'm going, too," Heather said.

"Follow orders," her father said. Not that he ever did. How else had he become who he was? But look at what it had cost him, especially now.

"Yes, dear," Patrice Sanger said, popping another pill. "Listen to your father." She smoothed down her silk pantsuit that had become wrinkled in the car. Removing her high-heeled shoes, she rubbed her toes, her pantyhose was making them itch.

Heather had the urge to jump out of the car and climb up the wildflower-lined hill, then run onto the bridge. She'd face the kidnapper and rip his face off if she had to, in an effort to get her little girl back.

She pressed her nose up against the car window and stared at the gray ocean, even the waves seemed violent as they splashed with fervor over the rocks and boulders. Out in the bay, she didn't see many boats, except for a few fishing boats and a tourist boat, probably headed out to Alcatraz. So where was her baby, her precious gift?

To the right through the fog, she could see the outline of the city in the distance. The panoramic view that normally brought her comfort, now only brought anxiety. How could the rest of the world go on when hers was so close to being over? Kiki had to be found . . . alive.

*   *   *

Lucky drove his Ferrari to the south entrance of the bridge, exiting just before the tollbooths into the upper parking lot above Fort Point. He saw no sign of cops or anything out of the ordinary. He parked, then went into the souvenir gift shop.

"Are the cops here, yet?" he asked a clerk.

"If your car's been broken into, we aren't responsible, but I can call security or the police, if you'd like."

"No, my car hasn't been broken into. Know what, never mind." She obviously didn't have any information. He looked down into the case by the counter then. Then pointed something out. "I'll take those."

Taking the binoculars, which were more like a toy, he stood at the edge of the sidewalk entrance onto the bridge. The weather was damp and breezy. "The baby must be cold," he said to no one. The feeling of helplessness was new to him. Watching and waiting was all he could do.

*   *   *

The kidnappers were in the parking lot on the north side of the bridge. "How's the kid doing?"

"Like you care? Don't worry, she's still alive."

"It was an unnecessary stop to get food. A stupid risk."

"She had to eat, a little formula. Thought it would quiet her down."

"I guess you know about these things."

"No, just instinct."

"When we walk onto the bridge, remember, no leaving the little shit until I verify the money transfer."

"We've run through the plan enough times. I've got the phone. When the money's in the account, we dump the screaming brat. Most importantly, remember, one screw up, and you're dead."

"I know, I know."

*   *   *

Kiki Marie didn't like the cold, strange hands that had finally picked her up. She didn't like the taste of the food that had come next. She didn't like the direction this new day had taken.

*   *   *

Robbie arrived at the Sanger residence, and one of the maids recognized him and okayed him into the house through security.

"What's happening?" he asked, running inside.

"They go get baby," the cook said, in broken English.

A police officer approached Robbie. "Who are you? And state your business."

"I'm Kiki's Godfather. Where are they?"

"I'm not at liberty to disclose that information."

"Like hell, you're not." On his way out of the house, he stopped briefly and glanced around. Cords, computers, telephones, Styrofoam coffee cups, half-eaten Danish and maps were strewn about. He leaned over and looked at one of the maps. The San Francisco Bay Area with a red circle drawn around one landmark in particular.

He ran out to the garage. The chauffeur was polishing the Rolls.

"How can you be doing that at a time like this?"

"Mr. Barnes. It's you. I guess you heard."

"This is just terrible. We have to do something."

"What can we do? I was just trying to keep busy." He'd been the driver for the Sanger family for decades. Watched little Heather grow up. Now, this just killed him.

"I'll give you something to do." Hopping in the front passenger seat of the Rolls. "Let's go," he said.

"I take direction from Mr. Sanger."

"Not, today, you don't."

"Why do you need me to drive?"

"You're a professional driver, and I'm in no mood—okay?"

"Okay, sir," he said, putting his cap on.

"How fast can you drive?" Robbie asked.

The two men were now bound by a mission. The old timer dressed in his uniform of gray slacks, white shirt, braided leather suspenders, and a cap. The youngster dressed in a black turtleneck and black jeans, with an earring in one ear and anxiety in his heart.

As they drove out down the long driveway, the chauffeur took his cap off, tossing it into the back seat. He'd always hated wearing that thing, only did so because Mr. Sanger had thought it was humorous.

As the Rolls merged onto the freeway, the driver crossed over to fast lane, and headed north toward the bridge.

*   *   *

The kidnappers got out of the car and walked on the bridge. The baby was in a stroller. At first glance, man, woman and child appeared to be nothing more than a family going on an outing, except that he had a loaded revolver in his pocket and she was overdue for her next heroin fix.

"Can he be trusted?"

"He came highly recommended. He's gonna pretend to have car trouble, stop briefly. We'll leave the kid on the bridge, then we'll hightail it into the car. It'll be so fast, they won't know what happened, just like the kid snatch. Another car will be waiting after we get across the bridge. From there, we'll go into the Sausalito harbor and a boat will be waiting. They'll never find us. The money will have been transferred into a secure account. We'll be home free. What a great country this is, the opportunities are endless."

"Let's get to the tower and get this over with," she said, patting down her hair. Hadn't put enough hair spray on it, her usual teased hair was flattening in the damp weather, and her high heel shoes were impractical to walk in. She hadn't realized the walk to millions would be so uncomfortable.

*   *   *

Lucky watched through the cheap binoculars, but hadn't seen anything that looked out of the ordinary. Where were the damn cops? The fog was still thick, making visibility difficult, but out of the corner of his eye, he saw a couple. They were pushing a baby stroller, but didn't look like typical parents. He adjusted the binoculars to get a better look. The man seemed older, perhaps a grandfather. Though it was foggy out, he appeared to be wearing sunglasses. He had something in his hand, probably a cell phone. The woman had red hair that she kept touching with one hand, then the other. She pushed the stroller as it swerved back and forth in the wind. The woman looked as if she were either drunk or walking with a limp. Lucky's eyes narrowed, and as the mismatched pair neared, he tried to bring them into better focus. The binoculars were no good. Tossing them aside, he edged closer. He needed to get a better look. A real look. His eyes were lying to him; the fog was playing tricks on his vision.

*   *   *

At the fort, the agent spoke into his wrist. "Everyone in place?"

At least ten agents quietly responded. Some hidden in the elevator in the tower, others posing as tourists, bridge workers in white coveralls were perched high in the air on platforms, going through the motions as if they were painting the bridge. They were all in place and ready.

Billy pressed the button on the laptop transferring the funds. If the kidnappers wanted the money, then the sooner they had it, the sooner this would all be over. Besides, it was a bogus transfer, the FBI had set it up to only appear real.

Heather couldn't contain herself. She jumped out of the car. "I'm going to the restroom," she told the cops.

Her father hopped out of the car after her. "I'm going with her, Patrice."

Patrice popped another tranquilizer and prayed her granddaughter would be found safe.

Heather glanced back. The agents were busy. She jogged over to the hill that led up to the bridge, keeping herself hidden from view. Glancing upward, she stopped and scanned the bridge. Her eyes were drawn to the activity on the bridge walkway. The heavy fog was thinning out, though not clearing completely. "Is that Lucky up there?" she asked.

"I knew it," Billy said.

Heather turned around. "Are you following me?"

"Of course, I am. And, yes, that looks like Lucky up there. I knew he was behind this, that bastard."

"Don't be asinine, I told him to meet us here."

"You don't know everything about him."

"Yes, I do. How dare you? He told me about being

attacked last night. By your henchmen, I suppose. Daddy, how could you?"

"Heather, darling. I was only trying to protect you. That's all I've ever tried to do."

"I've only wanted to live my own life, Daddy, mistakes and all."

"Are you saying Kiki Marie is a mistake?"

"No, I'm saying my not telling Lucky about her was a mistake."

"Well . . . this is one hell of a way for him to find out, don't you think?"

"Why don't these guys do something?" Heather asked, glancing back. Her patience was at a cracking point.

"Come with me, hon." Her father took her hand. He was going to get the kidnapper and rescue his granddaughter.

"Looks like we can get up there this way. Follow me." He led her up a dirt path that was steep, narrow, and filled with slippery, slimy rocks. At the end of the path was the upper parking lot. They assimilated in with a group of tourists getting off a tour bus.

"He's behind the tower," Heather said, pointing. "That must be Tower One, the turnover spot."

They blended in with the crowd and were only a few feet from the cars speeding by, unaware of what was happening.

                         *   *   *

Lucky hid behind the wide base of the tower. He peered around without the couple noticing. He could not believe it. This just couldn't be. A gush of fear splashed from his stomach to his heart. Was he seeing a ghost? The man was dead. Lucky knew this because after years of abuse, he had killed this bastard—regretting it later, but killed him nonetheless, or so he thought.

Then, the realization of who the woman was hit him. Her?

He glanced down at the stroller. Reality struck again, smack in the gut. His child. His kidnapped child.

Lucky tried to make sense of it. Why would they kidnap his child? Yeah, he'd made some money, but not that much. And, why hadn't they contacted him, the baby's father, for the ransom?

He only knew that he needed to take action to get his baby back. His and Heather's. The element of surprise would be in his favor. Lunging toward the stroller, Lucky tried to grab the baby, but was hit on the head from behind. He fell to the ground.

Billy stepped in and pushed the stroller away from the woman. "Get near me and die, sister," he said to the red-headed woman.

"Run, Daddy," Heather said.

Billy ran to safety with the baby, who was still in the stroller.

Lucky got up and swung an angry fist at the man that had struck him on the head. Hadn't been the first time they'd been in a fight, but it would be the last.

The agents, descending from their hidden identities, tried to thwart the kidnapper, but it was too late. He'd taken a hostage.

"Don't move, and I won't hurt her." Varic pushed the gun barrel into the side of Heather's neck.

Varic spoke in English, but his accent was the same as Lucky's.

"One step closer, and she gets a bullet through her neck and gets dumped over the bridge into the drink." He pressed her up against the railing. "It's a long fall."

The agents had to be careful, they couldn't take action with a weapon being held to Heather's head. They couldn't shoot him without risking her life. This would have to be played out with caution. The kidnapped victim was rescued but with a hostage. The game had only just begun.

"What do you want?" one of the agents asked. "Let's get

the cards on the table."

"I want to talk to this boy, here."

"Then, will you let her go?"

"Maybe."

Heather was rigid and shivered with fright, yet beads of sweat formed on her forehead. The time had arrived to face up to the pact she'd made. She'd made a deal with God, and now he was collecting.

"Well, well," the old man said to Lucky.

Lucky took a good look at the ghost from his past. His narrow eye was a slit into his evil soul. His skin was like rawhide. His eyebrows as bushy as his stubbly chin. The eye patch was still there, but had been pushed in the struggle to reveal the empty eye socket.

"Thought you killed me, huh?"

"Don't hurt me," she begged. The barrel of the gun was burning her skin.

"Shut up, you whore!" His grip on her tightened. "Aren't you a pretty thing? No wonder Lucky wanted to nail you."

"Don't talk to her that way," Lucky said.

"Is she too fragile? Can't handle real life? Been living in a shell her whole life?"

"Oh, please, let me go," Heather said. "We'll give you whatever you want." She kept telling herself to be calm, but her legs were trembling, about to give out.

"You know what I want? I want all your jewels. All your houses, all your cars, all your money." Then he laughed. "Oh, one more thing." He turned his attention to Lucky. "I have a few things to say to you. America's been good you, I see. You've made quite a bundle for yourself. But, the biggest bundle is your kid. A goldmine, I must say."

Lucky was in a daze. He couldn't get out of the state of shock he was buried under. The man, whose memory had haunted him for years had come back to haunt him yet again. This time to kidnap his child, and now threaten Heather's life.

But why?

"What's the matter? You surprised to see me?" he said, taunting Lucky. "To think, I always thought you'd amount to nothin', you bum."

"If I didn't kill you before, I surely will now," Lucky said, rage filling every muscle in his body.

An agent held Lucky back.

"Get back," the old guy said, "Or she's one dead Momma."

"Don't hurt her," Lucky said. "You said there were two things you wanted?"

"Oh, that. I guess I could've sent you an e-mail, but I think thanking someone in person is so much more personable, don't you?"

"I don't know what you're talking about. You're a raving madman."

"Now, that's no way to talk to your father."

"You're no father of mine."

"Don't be so rude. I wanted to thank you in person."

"For what?"

"For the headstone."

"How dare you denigrate my mother's memory by even speaking of her? This is between you and me. Leave her out of it."

Varic laughed, a sinister mocking sound that sent chills down Lucky's spine.

Heather shifted her body posture as she tried to free herself.

"Don't even think about it," he said.

"Let her go, she's done nothing to you. It's me you want. I'll give you whatever you want. Just let her go."

"Why? Is this little lady such a perfect Momma?"

Heather felt she might be able to escape, she could feel the gun shaking on her skin. He wasn't that strong of a man, she could probably struggle free, but she didn't want to die, either, taking such a chance. If he were going to kill her, anyway—

"She is a good mother," Lucky said, even though he'd just discovered she was a mother, he knew she would be a perfect one. "Just let her go." Lucky's skin crawled with hatred for this monster. His heart ached for Heather. All that he'd always run from, his abusive past was here and now, here and ready to squeeze the life from the only woman he could ever love this much.

"You wouldn't know a good mother if you saw one. Your mother was not the saint you thought her to be."

"Don't talk about her like that. I never even had a chance to know her."

"That's right, you didn't know her. You are the reason she is dead."

The words that had so many times replayed in Lucky's mind haunted him once again. He thought he'd committed murder, thought he'd killed this bastard of a father, but he hadn't.

"Let me tell you something about your Momma—"

". . . she loved me! And since she was dead, since I never had a mother, when I was a little boy, I prayed for my mother to come back to me. To protect me. When she didn't, I prayed for a father, one who would love me. A father to call me son. But, you. All you ever did was call me filthy names. The bottle was your first love. You hated me. Do you know how you hurt me?"

"So what if I was no saint? So what if I had a drink now and then? So what if I disciplined you on occasion?"

"You know what you did to me." The memory filled Lucky as if it just happened yesterday. He tried to forget, but it would never leave his soul. The pain was always there, hanging over his head, weighing him down

"Yeah, well, I had to deal with the likes of you. And, let me tell you a story about your Momma—"

". . . I don't want to hear it. Just let Heather go."

Heather's eyes welled, filling with fear. Everything seemed too quiet around her. The traffic had ceased. The cars on the bridge seemed to disappear. She'd seen her father take Kiki safely away. Thank God, at least she was safe.

"Why should I let her go?"

"I love her, but you wouldn't know about something as beautiful as love. You only know hate. I should've killed you. I wish I had the chance to try again."

"You tried, I will give you that." He dug the gun barrel further into Heather's neck, breaking the skin, causing it to bleed.

"Please, don't kill me," her voice, but a strained whisper from sheer terror and pain.

"Don't worry, Heather, he won't hurt you. He's too much a coward."

"You tried to kill me, now I'm going to kill her."

"You're crazy," Lucky said. "I never tried to kill you, it was self-defense. You tried to kill me for years, both physically and emotionally. And to think, after everything you've done to me, that I still felt sorry for you. You're right. I was crazy. I thought I'd killed you. I even called the cops, and they saved your evil life. What a mistake."

Lucky glanced over at the squirming accomplice, being held by a police officer. She was wearing a clinging sweater, tight pants, high heels and handcuffs. "Dina, how could you?"

"Love Bug," her voice was patronizing. "The way you left me, my hospital bills mounting, this was one trick I wanted in on. I had the collection agencies after me for my hospital bills, caused by you. When I met your old man here, we joined forces."

"Wasn't my fault that you fell down the stairs. I was only trying to help you. You were so drugged out you weren't able to so much as walk."

"That's a lie!"

"Dina, how could you kidnap a baby? My baby?" Lucky's eyes blazed flames at his father. "And you . . . how could you kidnap your own grandchild?"

He laughed, his sunken, dark eyes appearing deeply wicked. "That kid doesn't have one ounce of my blood in her."

"What are you talking about?"

"You don't get it, do you? You're stupid, like I always said you were—"

Bile came into Lucky's throat, and he tried not to vomit.

"I'm not your father," Varic said. "Your mother and her lover were killed in a car accident, not long after you were born. She'd left me a note saying she was leaving me, and taking you with her. The woman said something corny like it was important to her that her son had a father. But that I wasn't good enough, she said. That's when I learned that I wasn't your father. Her lover was your father. She said that she'd never even loved me. Just used me. She only married me 'cause her lover's divorce wouldn't be final till after you were born, and I was an easy mark. The two-timing bitch thought it was too scandalous in our village to have a bastard kid. On their way out of town, they got hit head-on. You were in the back seat. They both died, but you survived. I got stuck with you."

Lucky thought he loved his mother before, but now, he loved her even more. She'd tried to protect him from this evil man. And he didn't have his evil blood passed down to him, after all. He was now free and had to free Heather, but Varic wouldn't shut up.

"You were always a pain in the ass. I was glad when you took off. Then, when that fancy headstone appeared one day, it got me thinking about you, so I tracked you down. Didn't take me long. You didn't exactly cover your tracks. Got to New York, Dina had left word with the guys on the docks if you ever showed up again to get in touch with her. Seemed she had some bills and was rather irate with you."

"I went to Corky's, met Dina here. One night, some guy, called himself an actor, got drunk, and told this story about someone who called himself Lucky. How he didn't even know he had a baby, not to mention anything else about it. At first, I thought he was making the whole thing up, it was too incredible. But, Dina and I, well, we looked into it. The stupid kid didn't know it, but he led us right to you."

"I don't believe you," Lucky said.

"Speak of the devil, there he is."

Lucky turned around and saw Robbie.

Robbie felt a seizure coming on. The blood drained from his head.

"What's the matter?" Varic asked. "I think you walked into the wrong club that night."

"You son-of-a—" Robbie said, charging at him.

Varic and Robbie struggled, until Varic's gun discharged. Robbie was hit. The last thing in his mind before his body fell to the pavement was whether or not Heather would forgive him.

Next, Varic aimed the gun at Lucky, but a sharpshooter got Varic first.

Varic tottered at the railing and fell over the edge, hundreds of feet below, into the bay. He met with death.

Lucky ran to the railing and watched in relief and sorrow as the sea swallowed the man he had believed to be his father for so many years. Was it sorrow, or was it guilt? How could he feel anything for this man who'd made his life a living hell?

The paramedics split up. One ran to Robbie, while the other to Heather.

"I'm fine," she said. She nodded toward Robbie. "Please . . . please save him." Robbie, dear God, Robbie, please be okay, you have to be.

She glanced around.

"Where's my baby? Where is she?"

"Your father has her. She looks fine, but she should be taken to a doctor to be sure."

"Can someone bring her to me? I've gotta see her." One of the paramedics was cleaning the wound caused by the gun barrel, then bandaged it.

"You should be seen by a doctor too," the medic said.

"Later, besides, I'm fine," Heather said. Her injury was inside down on her heart, causing a terrible ache, but now it was for Robbie, her dearest and most loyal friend. Heather glanced over and watched as Dina was led away. Her rights being read to her in the process, she guessed.

"I'm just an innocent bystander," Dina protested. She was struggling with the tight grip around her arm.

"Save it for the judge," the cop said, putting her in the back of a squad car, pushing the mat of her red hair down in the process.

"Is he going to be okay?" Heather asked as the paramedics judged the severity of Robbie's gunshot wound.

"We don't know, yet." They stabilized him and lifted him onto a stretcher. "It might look worse than it is, ma'am." The paramedic seemed hopeful.

Lucky turned from the railing to join the crowd that had gathered around. "Robbie, can you hear me?" Lucky asked.

Robbie could hear him all right. Were these going to be the last words he ever heard. Lucky's?

Lucky leaned over him. "Man, I'm so sorry about everything. I've said some pretty rotten things to you in the past."

Robbie forced his eyes open. The rift was over. "It's okay." Then he closed his eyes. Through the confusion, he still knew that anything Lucky had said or done paled in comparison to his own mistakes.

Robbie's pain was unbearable until he felt a warmth come over him, and the pain suddenly vanished. The morphine had worked its way into his bloodstream. Then the medics carried the stretcher to the ambulance.

Heather followed alongside.

"The baby—" Robbie said, glancing up at her.

She wiped her tears away. "She's fine. My father carried her away to safety."

Robbie closed his eyes. He was groggy, but thankful that the baby was safe. "I'm so sorry." His voice was faint.

"Robbie, it's not your fault."

"Am I going to be . . . fired?" Robbie asked, his voice barely audible. With the mistakes he made, how could she ever forgive him?

The paramedics loaded him into the back of the ambulance.

Heather climbed into the ambulance and knelt beside him. He couldn't die, he just couldn't. She wondered what he was trying to say. "Fired, what are you talking about?"

"As Godfa—"

"Robbie—no, of course not." She was amazed at his sense of humor under such circumstances. No matter what, she still loved him, still wanted him in her and Kiki's lives . . . and in Lucky's.

"I'm sorry," he said. The expression on his face appeared peaceful.

"We're going to take him now, ma'am."

"Okay," Heather said to the paramedic. Heather kissed Robbie on his forehead. "I'll see you later."

Robbie tugged at the oxygen mask covering his face, he had to get the words out.

"Robbie, don't do that," Heather said.

But, he had to say the rest. "I . . . love . . . you . . . barefoot . . . gir—" Then his head dropped back, his eyes shut, and a deep sleep took over.

A warmth of love spread over her. She knew that Robbie was going to recover, she could feel it.

With its siren echoing across the bridge, the ambulance sped away out of view.

"I love you, too, Robert Barnes." A tear dropped onto the asphalt road.

In the distance, she saw her father approaching with the baby in his arms. Thank God. Soon, she would be back in her arms. She wanted to run to her infant, but first had some explaining to do to Lucky. Enough time had been lost already.

"How about you, me and the baby go see Robbie later?" Lucky asked.

"Lucky, I wanted to tell you so many times—"

"Doesn't matter now."

Lucky felt as if something had changed inside of him, a realignment of his soul. A rebirth, a creation of a whole new universe.

Heather felt the bandaged spot where moments before the gun had pierced her skin. Her face felt hot from all of the excitement, and the serious look she had was aimed at Lucky. "Lucky, your daughter's going to love you."

"Heather, I'm going to be there for her. Be a father, a good father as the man I'd wished for in a father, but never had. You know, I'd give anything for my child. I'd give my life."

"Lucky—" Heather said, hugging him. The words brought her comfort, vanishing any uncertainty. "Can you ever forgive me?"

He pulled back and whispered, "Heather, what are you talking about? I'm the one that begs forgiveness."

"I never told you about our baby. That wasn't right."

"I walked out on you, that wasn't right. If we went over our past wrongs, my past wrongs, it would take a lifetime."

"I know," she said. She felt just having him near, reinforced her own strength. As if he were the missing part of her life, the other half of her soul. They were two souls that had been lost, each searching for freedom and love. Destiny had brought them together, God brought a child, but then, for a dark while, they were lost in their uncertainties. Now destiny had brought them back together again.

"Heather, my love, I'm sorry about the past too. But, now, I'm ready to commit. To forever. That word used to scare me, but not anymore. Today is about letting go of the past, and tomorrow is about living for the future."

Tears of happiness streamed down her cheeks, much as an unexpected butterfly kiss.

"Heather, I love you."

"I love you, too."

Amidst the commotion of agents, cops and bystanders who were clicking away with their cameras, Lucky felt as if it were only he and Heather present. He got down on his right knee.

"Lucky . . . what are you doing?"

"Heather Kane, will you marry me?"

She hesitated, not out of uncertainty, but out of a desire to record this moment for eternity. "Of course, I will marry you."

He stood up, and they threw their arms around each other, not wanting to ever let go. His demons were gone, and he felt blessed. God had answered his prayers. Her fears were gone, and she felt blessed. God had answered her prayers. Even the ones that she'd been afraid to ask for.

Billy, who had been standing there, witnessed the love between his daughter and Lucky. He'd been so wrong about him.

He lifted his granddaughter to show Heather. The baby was asleep and wrapped in a blanket that the paramedics had provided after checking her for injuries.

Heather nodded to her father, then whispered into Lucky's ear. "Here's my dad, Lucky," she said.

Billy took his cue. With his free hand, he patted Lucky on the shoulder. "Excuse me. I'd thought you'd like to meet your daughter."

Lucky turned around. Not looking at Heather's father, he only saw his baby. His eyes never moved from her angelic face as he took her into his arms for the first time.

She had his dark hair, and Heather's perfect face. He leaned down and kissed her forehead. Her eyes opened as if acknowledging him. Tears formed, and his heart filled with joy. This was how fatherhood was supposed to feel. A man filled with love and only good things, that was fatherhood. In this single moment, holding his child, he felt as if all the loose ends in his life had just been cut free.

"She is a wonder, isn't she?" Billy asked.

For the first time, Lucky glanced up at the man. Him? His mouth gapped open, only no words came out. He glanced over to Heather, his eyes begging an explanation.

"Lucky, I'd like you to meet my father, Billy Sanger."

"I ... I ... don't know what to say."

Billy opened his arms to Lucky. "Let me just say welcome to the family."

Heather stepped back as she took in the sight of Lucky holding their child, and her father giving him a hug. She cast her eyes upward and thanked God.

"This is amazing," Lucky said. Turning from Billy, he glanced at Heather. She was gazing up at the sky with a faraway look. "Heather—"

It was as if the universe had taken a black hole and created a new galaxy. She could feel something, a presence, as if something or someone was observing them.

"Heather?"

She broke free from her trance, and looked at Lucky. "Did you say something?" She walked over to him, her body released from the pressing anxiety she'd felt only a short time ago.

"Your father is Billy Sanger?" he asked, astonished. "What else haven't you told me?" His voice was playful, teasing.

Heather laughed. She threw her head back, her hair glistening in the softness of the morning rays. Could life get any better? "Nothing, I promise." She put her hands to her face as if she'd just remembered something. "Well, there is one other thing."

"I knew it."

"I have a gift for you. A present."

"What else is there?"

"It's something that I've longed to give you forever, it seems." Heather smiled as she thought about the painting, and how thankful she was that it hadn't been damaged.

"Don't ever try and figure her out," Billy said, his voice light-hearted. "Just love her."

"That I do, sir. Count on it, Mr. Sanger."

"About last night," Billy said, his voice taking a serious tone, "Lucky, I'm so sorry my guys roughed you. I only wanted them to search the house, that's all. Please forgive me."

"So, those were your men? I thought they were going to snuff me out. Remind me to never get on your bad side."

Billy laughed. "I'll give you this much, you have a sense of humor."

"I think I just found it. Let's forget about it, okay?" Lucky asked. "The baby was found safe and sound. Heather's safe, Robbie is going to be fine. That's all that's important. Apologies and forgiveness, all across the board, is the name of the game today."

"I'm sorry," Billy repeated.

"Heather," Lucky said, glancing down at their child, "I just realized, I don't even know my own daughter's name."

"Kiki Marie."

"Marie?" he asked, as he tried to catch his breath. "That was my mother's name."

"I know," Heather said softly.

Tears trickled down Lucky's face. "How did you know?"

"Remember the photograph?"

The photograph. "Of course." Even torn and ragged, he always kept it near.

"Her name was written on the back."

Lucky nodded. "That's right." The tears came in a steady stream and passed his upper lip into his mouth.

"You don't mind that I named our daughter after her, do you?"

"Mind?" Lucky took a deep breath and tried to regain his composure. He motioned for Heather to take the baby. "Hold her a sec—" He reached into his pants pocket and pulled out his wallet. Wedged between his credit cards, a photo of Heather, and his California driver's license was a piece of paper that looked like a crumpled business card. His hand trembled as he unfolded it and tried to smooth out the wrinkles. "I still carry it," he said, handing it to her.

Heather hadn't seen the picture since Sea Breeze. Looking at it again, she thought she'd captured her presence in the portrait pretty well. Captured her beauty, her love, the essence of her soul.

Lucky wiped the moisture from his face and took the baby back into his waiting, fatherly arms. "I'm going to get the picture restored. For her." He nodded at the baby. She was crinkling her nose and pursing her lips.

"Actually," Heather said with a knowing smile, "there is something else." She was going to surprise him with it later, but this was the perfect moment to tell him about it.

"What is it?" Lucky asked. His thoughts were spinning as he tried to absorb every second of these moments that had changed his life forever. Heather, his baby, a new life.

"A portrait I did. I've been wanting to give it to you forever. I call it *Heritage*," Heather said. The title just came to her.

"Heritage?" He was only half-hearing what she was saying. "Portrait?"

"It's of your mother. I used the image from this picture as a guide," she explained.

Through his tear-clouded vision, he fixed onto Heather's eyes. Her love permeated to his very core. She knew him better than he knew himself. How had God ever sent him this angel? To fill an emptiness, a heartache he had only run from before. Then to be given a second chance with her, and now with their child, a chance to pass on the love he was now capable of giving as well as receiving.

Lucky and Heather kissed, their lips melted together as they rediscovered each other. It was an awakening that filled every fiber in their bodies. Two souls that had been lost were now found. Two souls that were meant to be together were. As if God had planned it that way. As if he had known all along.

Kiki Marie was getting restless. She squirmed in her father's arms.

Heather and Lucky changed their focus from each other to the child that they shared together. Heather leaned down and gave Kiki a kiss on her rosy cheek. "Mommy's right here," she said.

"I think she's getting hungry," Lucky said, with a proud smile on his face.

Billy put his hand on his growling stomach and rubbed it in a circular motion. "She's not the only one," he said in a joking manner. He approached Lucky and patted him on the shoulder and nodded to Heather. "What do you say we get off this bridge?"

"Is Mother still down at the fort?" Heather asked, as she wiped the tears from her face.

"Yeah, and she's probably gonna give us all hell for taking so long." Billy laughed.

Walking between her father who held her hand, and her soon-to-be husband, who held her child, Heather smiled. "Let's go home."

Billy smiled at his daughter. "You said it."

Before they left, they took one last look around. The fog had lifted, allowing the sun to give its healing warmth. Traffic on the bridge was starting again. The unmarked cars and squad cars were thinning out. Notes were being written for reports to be filed. A Coast Guard boat was at the spot where Varic's body had fallen. Robbie was probably at the hospital by now. They'd go visit him later.

Now, turning to Lucky, Billy smiled. "Come on, let's go home, Son."

Son. Did the man realize what the word directed at Lucky meant? Son.

"You don't mind if I call you that, do you?"

"No, not at all, sir. May I call you 'Dad?'" His voice choked up as tears built a dam in his throat.

"That would be fine by me."

Lucky glanced up at the sky. He could feel his mother's spirit looking down on them, and knew that she was smiling.

Acknowledgements

My mother, Dorothy Wall gave me my passion for reading, and my father, Cliff Wall, taught me to remember your heritage. I thank them with immense gratitude and love for all of their support.

I thank my sister, Beverly Rose Hopper, with whom I co-authored the book, Motherhood is not for Wimps, and who encouraged me from the beginning.

Thank you to Larry Wall and his creativity. His ability to think of new ideas and implement them is a gift.

Kathleen Russell is a talented artist, I have had the privilege of her designing the cover of Silicon Secrets, and I thank her from the bottom of my heart.

Thank you to my friends, with whom we have shared our lives, hopes and dreams.

I thank my sons, Tim Jr. and Daniel, who are enthusiastically supportive, and their strength and character, immeasurable. A truly lucky mom has such great men to call sons.

To Tim Sr., thank you for your support and love.

Love,
Catherine

About The Author

As a young child, Catherine Burr moved with her family from Canada to sun-drenched Northern California. With her siblings, she played in the orchards and open fields of Santa Clara Valley, cherishing the beauty of the land, until progress arrived in the name of Silicon Valley. When her father took her on a tour of an early Silicon Valley computer company, she was filled with intrigue, as the framework was being laid for the high tech generation, as well as ideas for Catherine's future novels.

When Catherine's children started college, she decided to fulfill her dream of writing fiction. Besides writing, she enjoys gardening, curling up with a good book, and the beach. Catherine is currently at work her next novel, a sequel to *Silicon Secrets*.

Visit Catherine's website at www.catherineburr.com.

 **NEW LINE PRESS**

To order additional copies
of this book or *Desires and Deceptions*

Visit the New Line Press website
www.newlinepress.com

Read Catherine Burr
Desires and Deceptions

The story of a young girl's journey into womanhood
and business venture that brings her to grips with her
romantic ambition and conflicting values.

Desires and Deceptions
Trade paperback
ISBN 1-892851-02-4

Money is a good servant but wealth becomes a cruel master when
Marisa's preference for living collide and meet her head on.
When big bucks are up for grabs are there no such thing as friends?

Dreams – Love – Money – Silicon Valley
Success is getting what you want. Happiness is wanting what you get.

Also Visit Catherine Burrs's website
www.catherineburr.com